A Hustler's Son

A Novel by T. Styles

This is a work of fiction. The authors have invented the characters. Any resemblance to actual persons, living or dead, is purely coincidental.

If you have purchased this book with a 'dull' or missing cover--You have possibly purchased an unauthorized or stolen book. Please immediately contact the publisher advising where, when and how you purchased this book.

Compilation and Introduction copyright © 2006 by
Triple Crown Publications
4449 Easton Way, 2nd Floor
Columbus, Ohio 43219
www.TripleCrownPublications.com

Library of Congress Control Number: 2005910628
ISBN: 0-9767894-9-3
ISBN 13: 978-0-9767894-9-9
Cover Design/Graphics: www.MarionDesigns.com
Author: T. Styles
Typesetting: Holscher Type and Design
Associate Editor: Cynthia Parker
Editor-in-Chief: Mia McPherson
Consulting: Vickie M. Stringer

Printed in the United States of America

Acknowledgements

First and foremost I'd like to thank God. God has taken me out of a lot of situations and a lot of dark places. He has carried me when I didn't have the strength to carry myself. I am because of Him, and only in Him can I find peace.

I'd like to thank my son Kajel. I know we joke all the time, but you really are the smartest and most handsome kid in the world. I am so proud of you. Don't base your dreams off of the shortcomings of others, if you reach far enough, you can attain anything your heart desires. I pray you find the meaning in my work. There's an ugly side to the world out there, that's unworthy of you. Avoid it, at all costs, and continue to follow the Lord; He'll guide you the right way.

I'd like to thank my mother. She has given me the strength that only a black woman can give. It's because of you, that one job was never enough for me. Thank you for believing in me no matter what! I love you.

To Charisse Washington, I don't think the world can rotate properly without you. Thanks for being my number one fan, critic and friend. I can do everything because of you. Whenever I woke up at 3 o'clock in the morning with a new chapter to read, you were always willing to listen. I am eternally grateful for you.

To Da'juan, don't worry, you'll find out who you are and when you do, look out world! I love you!

To my sisters Tina and Kavina and my nieces Bria and Destanee, I love you. Remember, the more beautiful you are, the smarter you should be. Never base your life on beauty, because it fades, but your intelligence can last a lifetime. To my nephew Darius, what's up with our book together? Let's get it crackin'! I love you.

To my cousin Carlos aka Peanut, Billy, Dee and my favorite aunt, Paula!! Thanks for loving me regardless. It means so much to me.

To Tammy of Triple Crown, what can I say? You saw the value in my work before anyone else. Thank you for believing in me. This one's for you.

To Vickie Stringer. Where do I start? Thanks for Crowning me and for holding the Urban World down with a skirt! You're showing these men that we can run a business too! I am happy to be a part of your team, and thank you for giving me a chance. Don't worry, I won't let you down.

To my editor Cynthia. You are phenomenal! I am very, very happy that out of all the editors, they chose someone I was TOTALLY in tune with for my first TCP project. We worked like Salt and Pepper together. You were a remarkable contributor who did far more than just edit my book, you believed in it. Thank you. I look forward to our future projects together! And most of all, I look forward to your first big hit!

To the entire Triple Crown Family, without a team, there can be no company. With that being said, I appreciate everything that you did to put my book into print. I look forward to bringing Triple Crown another bestseller!

To Kalisha, from one talented sister to another, your time is coming. When it's all said and done, you'll have everything you deserve and everything your heart desires. I love you girl!! Keep your head up.

To Cece, keep writing! Don't give up and don't get distracted, it's not easy, but the reward is unprecedented. I love you.

Special thanks to my other friends, Marla, Allyn, Kristina, Cochise, Monica, Mona, Chaneta, Wood, Mr. and Mrs. Gross, Mark, Michael, and George Valentine.

To my readers, this novel is different than what I've written before. But I pray that you can still see the creativity in my work. Street lit writing is an area few writers dare not touch. But I do so to become the voice for those who want their stories told accurately, and with as much passion as possible. Not telling the story doesn't hide the lifestyle nor does it make it go away. But if it's accounted for properly by authors like myself and other Triple Crown novelists, maybe we can move closer to a place of revelation. If nothing else, we can understand how they live, and appreciate our families and the lives we lead everyday.

What I'm feeling now. These people inspire me whether musically or mentally and to you I'd like to say Thank you. Janet Jackson, Sean Puffy Combs, Raheem Davaughn, Floetry, Jamie Foxx, Oprah Winfrey, Tyra Banks, Lil Kim, 50 Cent, Mariah Carey, Maxwell, R.Kelly and many others.

To anyone I may have forgotten to thank or mention, hold it to my mind and not my heart. P.S. Remember ... Dreams will remain dreams until you make them realities.

Email me at toysstyles@yahoo.com

Triple Crown Publications presents . . .

Janet
Chapter 1
September 16
Friday, 3:00 am

My hand was moving all over my body – over my breasts, along my thighs and between my legs. While it felt good, I wasn't doing it to reach an orgasm; I was doing it to put myself to sleep. I just got off work and was tired. All I wanted to do was close my eyes. Still, I appreciated the feel of my body even if nobody else did. I kept my body soft and I was complimented all the time on my caramel colored skin, and the short curly hairstyle I sported. With one hand on my breasts and the other between my legs, I was five seconds from reaching an orgasm. *Ummm. Ummm,* and then I heard it.

I sat up straight in bed to be sure I heard knocking at my front door. *Knock Knock Knock!* Who the fuck was that? I knew my son was home because I told him to get off the phone when I got in earlier. I grabbed my robe and walked toward the door. *Knock Knock Knock!*

I can't stand when a muthafucka knocks on your door at 3 o'clock in the morning. It usually means somebody died or somebody wants something. Either way, I didn't want to be bothered.

I grabbed the bat I kept next to my leather sofa and walked toward the door. I wasn't sure if I would be able to defend

1

myself with it if there was actually a barrel to my face, but I was certainly willing to try.

"Who is it?!"

"It's me! Let me in so I can talk to you. This shit has gone on too long."

"No! I'm not dealing with this shit no more! I'm serious, Delonte. Now get the fuck away from my door!"

"Baby, please don't do this shit to me! It's not what you think it is!"

"I know you better get from in front of my fucking door, before my neighbors start complaining and shit!"

"I got something for you, Janet. Please let me in so I can give it to you and then I'll leave. I promise."

Everything in me wanted to have enough strength to walk back to my room, but I loved him. As sorry as he was, I loved everything about him. I knew the moment I opened the door, he'd be trying to fuck me or something like that. It made me mad as hell that I still wanted him. It wasn't all about sex, because I could satisfy myself if I wanted to.

What I cared about was having a man lie next to me every night and have him still be there in the morning. Sometimes I ain't even feel like a woman unless a man was in my bed. To me, there was nothing more comforting than a man holding me and telling me he loved me, even if he didn't. I needed, and wanted, that type of *security* in my life, and only a man could give it to me. Especially considering the life I led and the nightmares that still haunted me.

That's how I got tied up with Lorenzo Davis in high school. He was my son's father and was never any good. He wouldn't even deal with me unless I arranged for him to sleep with my best friend Shelly Hall, and me, at the same time. And I did. Anything for Lorenzo was all I could think of, and believe me, making that arrangement was easy because Shelly looked at him like he was hers from the start. She didn't want to share him, she wanted to own him.

She loved fast cars and fast money. Lorenzo had both and loved showing them off. He used to run with Rayful Edmond in 1988 so back then, money wasn't a problem. He had enough to take care of me and her and whomever else came along. Although he's not dealing coke anymore due to being on lock down for 10 years, he still had a game that kept him paid.

I hated the day I ever invited Shelly into our bed. I would have never guessed she'd turn on me like that. She was supposed to want him only when I wanted her to. She was supposed to be a toy we could use and turn off when the game was over, but she developed feelings. Whenever I had my back turned, Shelly was smiling in his face and finding some way to touch him. She eventually became number one, and I became number two.

I don't know why I stayed with Lorenzo, except I wanted somebody to love me and call me theirs, and he did. He said he would protect me, if I was willing to do anything for him, and I did it all. From whooping his sister's ass for stealing his stash one day when he was locked up overnight, to keeping an eye on his mother when he was doing the stretch, I proved over and over that I was down for him.

To top it all off, there aren't many women who can say they got pregnant at the same time, in the same bed and with the same man as their best friend, but I can. To this day, it hurts looking at Shelly's son, Lorenzo Jr., knowing that he's Kelsi's brother, and remembering how they were conceived. I did everything for that nigga including sharing my bed and my body with another woman. When he got out of jail, he left me, left us, and Kelsi was only 5 years old.

He comes by and takes care of both of our kids. Shelly and I have remained cordial over the years but I hold a lot of resentment because I feel like she should have refused Lorenzo's advancements. Even though we were both 15 years old and didn't know any better, she was my best friend and knew I loved him. Whenever we talk about it now, although few and far between, she says she did it for me. *"I did it cuz you asked me to, Janet, and in the process, I fell in love."* I know that's not true because she was fuckin' him plenty of times I ain't ask the bitch to do shit.

I think what makes me maddest is that to this day, he sleeps with her when he's not with his wife. I don't know if I'm angry about her still being available to him, or him being available to her, but maybe sometimes second best is better than nothing at all.

"Baby, please open this door. We gotta talk. You got me out here looking like half of a faggot!"

Before I could say yes, he was banging on the door again. He was having a fit because I was always accessible to him, and because of it, he wanted shit when he wanted it. I don't know if I spoiled him or if his mama did. Hell, maybe it was both of us, but I was desperately trying *not* to give in so easy this time. Delonte went overboard, way overboard. I found out that the one person I trusted him around, his cousin Kenosha, he may have been sleeping with.

"Delonte, get the fuck from in front of my door, now! It's over!" I yelled. My voice was saying different things than my heart felt. I wanted him to fight for me and to fight for our relationship. If he truly loved me, he wouldn't leave despite what I told him.

"Naw it ain't over 'til the fuck I say it's over! Now open this fucking door, Janet!! This is my apartment, too! I still got my shit in there!"

"I packed up all your shit and took it to your mama's house, so go see her! This fuckin' apartment is in my name!"

4

A Hustler's Son

Although I wanted to be with him, he was breaking me down. Every other month I had to deal with a new girl in our lives. I couldn't trust him for shit and each time I took him back, I desperately tried to. Being alone is something I didn't want to do. I didn't want to be alone with myself or alone with my past. When my mama died five years ago, I lost the last person who truly cared about me. I had nothing and nobody except Kelsi back then, and he was only 10 years old.

On the day of my mother's funeral I met Delonte. I thought he was given to me from God. He knew I was alone, because I prayed to Him every night about it. I thought he was sent to help me get over all of the things that I'd lost. He said all the right things at all the right times. *"Janet, you don't ever have to worry about anything. You and Kelsi will be taken care of, baby. Trust me."* And I did. I believed in everything he said, even though my *past* reminded me that people aren't always what they seem.

"Ma, who's at the door?"

When I turned around I saw my 15-year-old son Kelsi towering over me. I noticed a lot about him over the past few years besides his physical changes. One of the main things I noticed was that the little boy I was raising was slowly changing into a man. He was still respectful, but his line of questioning had drastically changed. He went from *"Can I go outside and play?"* to *"Who's dude, Ma?"* and, *"What he want with you?"*

"K-man, get back to bed, it's a school night," I said as I turned around to face him.

"I can't go back to sleep with all that bangin' and yellin' going on. Who is that at the door, Ma?" he asked, looking into my eyes.

"It's Delonte, now take your ass back to bed. I'm not playing," I responded, trying to regain authority. After all, I was the parent, not him. Why was he giving me the third degree?

Kelsi looked at me and shook his head. I could tell he did-

5

n't appreciate Delonte disrespecting what he playfully referred to as *his* house. My baby had definitely evolved and it was fucking me up a little. He was no longer fearful of me but he never got out of line. I was OK with that because I wasn't raising no punk. I was trying to raise a man and as long as he stayed in his place, we weren't going to have any problems.

"OK, Ma. Let me know if you need me," he said as he kissed me on my cheek.

"I will baby."

He walked back toward his bedroom dragging his feet. There he was, 15 years old and already over six feet tall. He had what I referred to as boy muscles. I say that because most boys were naturally strong, and if they did their bodies right, their muscles would show. Now, *every* muscle in Kelsi's body was already defined, just like his father.

He had a six pack, pecs, biceps and all that other shit, too. I stayed chasing these fast-ass little girls away from my house, but as you know, there's always *one* who gets through. Kelsi looked more like a man in his white wifebeater and gray cotton boxers than a child. He even had a little mustache and chin hair that he kept neatly trimmed along with his low haircut that was always shaped up.

When he was out of sight, I directed my attention back to the door. I stood on my tippy toes and looked out the peephole. He was still there, waiting. I also noticed that he had quieted down a little and stopped banging on the door. I knew it was because he heard Kelsi ask me who it was.

Delonte also realized K-man was growing and wasn't a kid anymore because we had several conversations about him in the past. I didn't want to say anything, but I knew Delonte feared him a little. After all, some of the shit he did to me was just plain wrong and if K-man were a little bit older, he would have whooped his ass a long time ago.

"Baby, I know you're there. Open the door … pleeease," Delonte begged in a voice loud enough for me to hear.

I unlocked the door, placed the bat next to the couch and sat down. I grabbed the remote control and thumbed through the channels. A few seconds later, Delonte slid in wearing a pair of Sean John jeans and an oversized plain white T-shirt. As usual, he had on a fresh pair of butters and a black cap pulled down, partially covering his eyes.

"What you watching, baby?" he asked as he stood next to the couch. He made me mad trying to play me like everything was OK. It won't be that easy, nigga.

"Look, this TV's watching me, now what the fuck you want?!"

"You know what the fuck I want. I want to come home, baby," he whispered as loud as he could without K-man hearing him. "And I know you want me, too."

"Do you really think I'll take you back after catching you fucking your cousin? That is so fucking nasty anyway. I should slap the fuck out of you right now, Delonte!"

"Go ahead baby, slap me if that makes you feel better, but what if you're wrong?"

There he goes with that shit again. Whenever I caught Delonte in a lie or something he shouldn't be doing, he'd ask me, "But what if you're wrong?" It was the stupidest question I've ever heard and the only thing it did was prove his guilt. Anyway, I saw him engaged in a full-fledged kiss with his cousin right in front of his aunt's house off of Clay Street in Northeast, D.C. Not only did they live in the same neighborhood, they lived on the same street, which made matters worse. He spent a lot of time with Kenosha when he wasn't with me. For him to be a 32-year-old man, I thought that was a little weird, but she played me close by kissing my ass whenever he was around.

"Delonte, I caught you in *her* car, kissing her. Don't fucking lie to me!"

The truth was I didn't care what he said because I saw it with my own eyes. It was no longer a question whether or not he was telling the truth, everything now depended on how *good* the lie he told was.

I've played this game with Delonte for awhile now. I was becoming strong enough to handle the lies but too weak to live without him. I was no longer afraid of catching him in a lie and not wanting him. I was afraid of catching him in a lie and him not wanting me.

"Hear me out, Janet. Kenosha had broken up with that punk-ass nigga she was fucking with over there on Clay. She was drinking and shit, I was walking out of my mama's house to go check on my aunt, when I saw her in the car crying. You know she my favorite cousin, so you know me, I jumped in the car ready to kill somebody for laying their hands on her. She started crying and told me what happened. I was only hugging her because she was upset. She wrapped her arms around me and –"

"You decided to fuck her?!" I yelled, just a little bit louder than I should have.

"No baby, I ain't fuck her," he said calmly. He sat down on the couch beside me, taking off his cap and smoothing his hair with his hands.

I was frustrating him and I was pleased. If you gonna lie, at least make it a good-ass lie, damn! I already hated how the entire family lived on the same block, so now I would have to worry about what he was *really* doin' when he went home and whose home he was really at.

"Baby please, just hear me out. I know how it looked and all, but tell me what the fuck I look like fucking my baby cousin? She's a kid, man!!"

"First off you're only 32 and she's 25 so the age difference is not that significant nigga so don't even try it. You say all the time how those Clay Street niggas stay sweatin' Kenosha, so I know you think she's attractive, and now you saying 25 years old is too young for you to fuck? Don't forget you fucked one younger than that last year Delonte, and she was only 21."

"Why you bringin' up old shit? I'm telling you that I didn't fuck my fucking cousin, J! What the hell is wrong with you?"

When I heard a door creek, I knew K-man was up again. He would probably make his way to the kitchen or something like that to see what was going on. Lately, he was extremely over-protective of me and Delonte knew it, too.

Delonte sat back on the couch and took the remote out of my hands. We both pretended to be glued to the TV, which before Delonte turned, was on some Spanish speaking channel.

"Kelsi, I thought I told you to go back to bed!"

"I am, Ma, I'm just thirsty that's all," he said while looking at Delonte.

"K, it's a school night and it's almost time for you to get up," I said, feeling he wasn't threatened enough.

"I know, Ma, but I can barely sleep," he said as he cut his eyes back at Delonte.

"Hey K-man, what up? You gonna check out the Giants and Falcons on Sunday? It's gon' be sweet! Vick ain't got nothin' on Testaverde. It's ole school against new school, boye!"

Delonte was trying to ease the tension in the air but Kelsi didn't respond and disappeared into the kitchen. Delonte looked at me and shook his head. Kelsi had never been disrespectful to any of my friends but he was tonight. It was as if my little boy had gone to sleep forever and was replaced with a grown-ass man.

"You know that boy is starting to smell himself," Delonte whispered. "I'm gonna have to check that little nigga one day,

I'm telling you," he said as he placed the remote control down on the glass table. "If his daddy won't do it, I ain't got no problems with it."

"Don't worry about K, you need to be worried about yourself and convincing me why I should let your sorry ass come back."

Delonte took a deep breath and grabbed one of my hands. "Baby, I love you and I wouldn't do anything like that. I ain't got nowhere else I want to be besides with you." Kissing my hands, he continued, "Now I know I fucked up in the past and I'm sorry. But what you saw was me consoling my baby cousin, after that weak-ass nigga dumped her and that's it. You know how close we are, J."

"Yeah, but I didn't know *how* close, Delonte. Talk about kissin' cousins, your mouth was covering hers like you were breathin' new life into her with her skanky ass. And what boyfriend you talking 'bout? How come I ain't never seen this mysterious boyfriend?" I whispered. "Aren't you the least bit embarrassed?"

"I'm not embarrassed because I know what really happened and it wasn't how it looked. I know what I was doing but if you saw her kissing someone, it wasn't me. Besides, you ain't got no reason to be seeing her boyfriend cuz he ain't your man."

"Well she seeing mine every night," I spat back with an attitude, not even caring how stupid I sounded.

He sat back on the sofa and folded his arms and continued with his groveling. "You have to start trusting me, baby. I mean … I cheated a few times, but after the last time, I haven't stepped out on you again. I swear to God, baby. I fucking love you, girl!"

"I'm a woman, Delonte. That's your problem. You don't know the difference."

He took another deep breath as if to ignore my last comment. "You tell me right now. Do you want me to leave or stay?" He sat up straight and looked me in my eyes.

I hated when he did that, turn the shit back on me. It's always easier to take him back because he begged, than it was because I wanted him. He knew I wanted him home and he knew the game we played was only temporary. I'm sure Delonte was as aware of my insecurities and fear of being alone as I was. I paused. I couldn't answer the question right away. To answer right now would mean he'd do whatever he wanted to tomorrow. Why couldn't he find happiness with me and our relationship? Why couldn't I be enough for him?!

What scared me was that he could look me straight in my face and lie just like my ex-boyfriend, Jarvis. I glanced over his chocolate-covered skin and smiled inside. *Damn you're fine,* I thought to myself.

"Janet, did you hear me?"

"I heard you and I'm thinking," I said as I looked toward the kitchen to see if Kelsi had come out yet and also trying to buy more time. I couldn't appear too anxious. *Damn, Delonte.* Why did he have to ruin our relationship like this and force me to admit my weaknesses by saying I wanted him back?

"I'm a grown man and as much as I can't see living my life without you, I'll leave if that's the way you want it," he said, growing impatient with my silence.

I looked at Delonte's fine ass like I was really thinking about not taking him back … *again*, but my mind was already made up the moment I unlocked the door. I needed him and I knew he needed me. I also knew that taking him back wouldn't be the last time I would have to put his ass out but I didn't want another woman having him, even if the other woman was his cousin.

He was an attention magnet. Delonte was 5'11", dark-skinned and kept his hair cut really low and neat. He was told

quite often that he resembled Morris Chestnut. He played bas-
ketball every day at the Gold's Gym in Beltway Plaza in
Greenbelt, Maryland so he was toned, athletic and could run
this 5'7", 140 pound frame all over this apartment. I often wondered if he weren't so attractive, if our relationship would be
better, but then, would I even want him?

Before I could say anything, Kelsi walked out of the kitchen
holding a cup and a piece of cake I made yesterday. I told that
boy time and time again *not* to eat in his room because it attracted roaches, and there he was taking food out of the kitchen and
into his bedroom. As I looked at him, I started to say something
but the look in his eyes caught my attention. I could tell he was
getting ready to say something but I didn't know what to expect.
There was fire in his eyes and he looked as if he wanted to rip
Delonte's throat out, so needless to say, I was going to let the
cake thing slide. At least for now.

"Delonte, maybe you should talk a little lower when you
makin' comments, man. Feel me?" Kelsi said in a calm but serious voice, in between chewing a piece of the cake.

I sat there frozen and speechless. My feet wouldn't move
and neither would my mouth. If he was bold enough to talk to
Delonte that way, who knew what else he might say. K-man just
treated Delonte like he was one of his friends right in my face.

"Uh, K, don't be disrespectful to Delonte, it's not right," is
all I could manage to say to him.

"Sorry Ma, but I'm not the one knocking on the door at 3
o'clock in the morning begging. He is."

"Little man, you got it all messed up. I love your mother and
my coming over here at *whatever time* is our business. Stay in
your place, youngin'."

Kelsi just laughed and walked toward his bedroom. Before
going into his room, he turned around and said, "Man, Atlanta
gonna crush the Giants. Testaverde's old, too old to be playing

anybody's ball. Oops, that's your team, my bad." Kelsi grinned devilishly and continued, "Vick, let's just say, he schoolin' them ole timers. By the time he through with them, they'll be beggin for the pain to stop. Youngstas is where it's at playa … unless ya'll old schoolers can handle a BEAT DOWN!" He turned around, walked to his room and closed the door. Cake and all.

I didn't know what to say to Delonte because truthfully, I was wondering what was going on in Kelsi's mind. He was a Sophomore in high school and I knew girls and the pressures of the world were already on his shoulders. Ever since last year, he had changed and there appeared to be extra weight he was carrying around all the time. I tried to make it easier by not sweating him with small stuff, but I didn't know if it was working. Maybe that was the reason he reacted the way he did to Delonte. Maybe I wasn't hard enough on him. Maybe I let him get away with too much. I had a feeling that he overheard everything Delonte and I were going through, and was tired of it, just like I was. Honestly, I didn't know what was going on with him, and I felt useless as a mother. I found myself thinking only of Kelsi, until Delonte started talking.

"Janet, what's up with K? He's really getting out of control and I'm gonna have to put him in his place sooner or later. What the fuck was that suppose to mean about the Giants getting BEAT DOWN? Was he threatening me?"

"Delonte please," I said as if he were boring me. "We have other things to worry about then some damn-ass football! *Anyway*, he's my son and I can handle him."

"So what you sayin'? If I live here I have to deal with the little nigga treating me like I'm a bitch? If that's what you sayin', Janet, I might as well roll right now."

"I'm not sayin' that, Delonte," I sighed as I took a deep breath.

He was acting like a kid, Kelsi was acting like my father,

and I was mad as hell. For one second I wanted both of them the hell out of my house! Nobody seemed to care that I had two jobs, one as a housekeeper and the other as a waitress and I was tired, mentally and physically.

"Just let me handle K-man. He has a few things going on at school and maybe he took it out on you. You know he likes you."

Delonte kissed me on my cheek and then softly on my lips. My acknowledgment of his feelings about how K-man treated him gave him confirmation that it was OK to move back in. And in a way, that made it easier for me, too. I really didn't feel like saying, *"Yes baby, I want you and need you to come back home."*

"I love you, Janet," he said as he kissed me. "I'm gonna grab my stuff and I'll be here by the time you get home from work. And quit that second job, baby, I don't want you working yourself to death. How you gonna take care of me?"

"I'll think about it, Delonte, but for right now, the money is good."

Delonte had been trying to get me to quit my second job forever. Every time I mentioned it, we'd get into another fight. Anyway, I worked the second job to look out for K-man, not for Delonte. I told Delonte I worked two jobs because I wasn't sure if we would make it, and I wanted to cover my bills, but that wasn't entirely true. The Sheraton paid all of our bills but I wanted my baby to have some of the things boys his age wanted so he wouldn't get too caught up in the streets. Unfortunately, I knew there was some shit I just couldn't keep him away from.

"Well, think about it a little harder. I get tired of living here and having you gone all the time," he said as he stood up and walked toward the door.

"Delonte, don't leave," I said as I followed him. "Stay with me until I leave for work. You can move your things in later."

"I can't, baby," he said as he opened the door. "But I'll be waiting for you when you get back," he continued as he kissed me.

"OK," I responded all disappointed. "I'll see you later."

"Aren't you forgetting something?" he asked with a sly smile on his face.

"Oh," I responded as I reached in and gave him a kiss.

"That was nice, baby, but I'm talking about my keys."

"Oh, I'm sorry, D, give me a second."

I forgot I snatched his keys when I put him out last week. I put him out six times already and each time the locks changed before the door slammed behind his ass, but I knew he was comin' back. That changing locks shit got expensive, so this time when I put him out, I snatched his shit.

I walked to the kitchen and opened the drawer where I kept them. They weren't there. I moved stuff around, took stuff out, and still couldn't find them. Then it dawned on me, *K-man has them.* Was he that dead-set on Delonte not moving back in that he would take his keys? I didn't want to knock on his door and ask him for them, because Delonte would know there was an even bigger problem with Kelsi than we realized.

"Baby, I left them at work. K-man will let you in later," I yelled from the kitchen where he could still see me.

He looked at me and said, "You sure? I don't want no shit when I come back home with all my stuff."

"I'm sure, baby," I said as I walked over to him at the door. "Now aren't you forgetting something?" I asked.

"Oh yeah," he said as he reached in his pocket, peeled off three crispy one hundred dollar bills and handed them to me.

I moved my fingers as if to say, *"Keep peeling, muthafuc-ka."* By the time he finished turning the pages, he'd paid the price of a cool grand to move back home. So far, it was the highest price yet.

"OK. I'll see you later. Don't forget to tell Kelsi I'll be here around five."

"I won't," I said as I kissed him and locked the door.

Kelsi
Chapter 2
September 16
Friday, 7:45 am

You can only push a person so far, until the person you pushed ceases to exist. That's what happened to me last year and had been happening ever since we moved to Autumn Woods, which used to be called Mattapony Apartments, about six years ago. *Stop crying, Kelsi! Never let them see you cry,* my Moms used to tell me. So what did I do? I stopped crying and stopped showing any kind of emotion in the face of these muthafuckas out here. I hardened up and hardened up quick. People looked at me and called me a boy, but I knew that lil' nigga left a long time ago. He had to. If he hung around any longer, he would have gotten us both killed.

My stompin' grounds bred criminals and I was no exception. I knew the mind made you vicious, not the work you put in, and I had been building myself up to put in work a long time ago. If it wasn't to protect myself, it would be to protect my Moms. Too many dudes had used her and I was tired of that shit. Every time she cried, I made sure I saw the tears fall from her face. That fueled my hate! When you've seen your Moms cry enough times, nothing else can fuck with you, especially if you feel you *can't* protect her, but I don't feel that way anymore.

I was the only man my Moms needed, the only man we

needed. I had plans to get us out of Autumn Woods so she wouldn't have to work two jobs. Even if I had to hustle a minute to build up our funds, I was willing to do *whatever* I had to do. *A man ain't shit unless he can take care of his family, Kelsi,* is what she used to tell me. *Man up or them streets will eat you alive.* Drugs and crime were my neighbors, and she told me to stay away, but I had plans to make them our means of survival.

I already knew the streets by name. By hustling on the side, I saved up about 15 grand and managed to keep her from finding out. That's cuz I watched niggas' games before I jumped in head first. I was quiet and let the streets tell me who to fuck with and who was on crud time. Before doing anything, I made sure K-man, the youngin', wasn't approaching anybody askin' to be put on, instead it was Kelsi, the man. I made sure my heart was in it, and when it was, I didn't approach the hand-to-hand cats because they were hungry just like me. I approached Skully, the meanest but most respected dealer in the hood. He respected my boldness and I've been workin' for him ever since.

Although I'm 15, I worked on myself, inside and out. I got my weight up and wiped the stupid smile off my face. It seemed like some people took pleasure in me being young and shit. They liked takin' their problems out on me, like I didn't have enough problems of my own. I was quiet and timid until I learned that being timid made you a target. The moment I changed, people respected me, except for two muthafuckas.

"So this nigga gonna tell my Moms I'm smelling myself. Bricks, I'm telling you right now, I was five seconds from breaking that nigga's jaw."

We were on our way to school and I was telling my boy what happened last night. Still tired, I was furious when I thought about it being because of Delonte's punk ass. I hated that dude with a passion!

The cold air eased me up a little, as each step caused the

wind to hit my face. I pulled my cap down further over my head, but it wasn't doing shit. Good thing I grabbed my gray hoodie and wore two shirts underneath it. I also had on jeans and my Timbs, which never came off. Whenever they got scuffed, I just replaced them. I knew Bricks was cold because he had on two short-sleeved T-shirts and was walking with his hands in his pockets. He was strutting at first like it really wasn't cold, but right before we reached the school, he was shakin' like a crack-head.

"You should have, *Kells*. You should have broke that nigga down. That's your fucking house, man."

"Naw … I'ma let the nigga breathe for now. My Moms is feelin' him and I can't break down *every* nigga that's feeling her, at least not now anyway. But I fucked his head up with that Giants shit."

"You wild!" He laughed. "But you know I ain't feelin that shit. I fucks with the Giants, too."

"Yeah well, fuck that shit! Last Monday night they got they ass whooped, it's just as simple as that. It was on time too because I wanted him to know he could get beat down just like them niggas if he disrespected my Moms."

"You think he got the message?" Bricks asked, sensing my hate.

"I don't know, but I know my Moms picked up on it."

"How you know?"

"Cuz I ain't realize I had cake in my hand when I walked in my room."

"What that mean?" he asked, clueless. Sometimes you had to explain shit to Bricks like he's in pre-school.

"Nigga, my Moms never let me eat in my damn room. She had to be fucked up behind that shit."

"Oh … I feel you. Well, did you tell her about Black's party tomorrow night?"

"I ain't ask her yet. It won't be a problem though because Delonte is back. She be all happy and shit when he comes home. That was the only reason I didn't steal him in his face last night, no matter how I felt about him."

Did I already say I hated Delonte? We used to be cool but lately, he'd done one too many things to my Moms. Between the yelling and the fighting he made me despise his ass. Every time I smelled that bamma's cologne, I wanted to kill him, and I mean that shit. I loved my Moms to death and I knew if she knew how I felt, she'd be all fucked up, so I never said shit.

"Well make sure you ask her because mad bitches gonna be there tomorrow."

"Oh don't even worry about that nigga. I *will* be telling her the moment I get home tonight."

"Whatever nigga."

"Why you say that?"

"Because. What's up with you and Lakeisha? Ain't ya'll fucking tonight?"

"OK why you clocking the work my dick be putting in?" I laughed.

"Fuck you, man. You know what I mean, ain't she coming through tonight?"

"Yeah nigga but I ain't no marathon runner! I ain't fucking her *all* night! We make it to my place by three and Moms don't get in until nine."

"Damn that girl *fyne*! Whatever happened to it ain't no fun if the homies can't have none?" Bricks laughed.

"I'm telling you right now, don't get fucked up before first period."

Bricks was cracking jokes, but he was right, Lakeisha was a dime for real. I met her when we were both Freshmen at Bladensburg High last year. I knew at that moment, she'd be my girl. She was kickin' it with Charles Rick, whose face had been slashed from the bottom of his left eye to his chin but the nigga was weak. It would only be a matter of time before she would kick him to the curb. True to my word, before the end of the year, she was mine.

She was my type of girl, redbone, 5'5" and thick as all get out. She even had that soft hair because her mother was Spanish and her father was black. She had a lot of niggas on her shit and although I was checkin' her out, I did it from afar at first. Anyway I knew she'd come to me because her man was weak. He was the only dude in the 12th grade still asking girls if he could have a chance. I just fell back until that nigga's weak-ass game wore out, and by May, that's exactly what happened.

I still remember that day. School had just let out and it was hotter than Africa outside. Me, Bricks and a few of my other boys were on our way to get banana shakes from Checkers, a restaurant not too far from school. I hated going to the counter asking for a banana milkshake, so I used to give Bricks my money to order both of ours. One day I may tell him I sent him to the counter all those times on some punk shit to order my shakes, but he ain't never seem to care, so why should I?

Anyway, Lakeisha walked up to me when we were almost there.

"K-man!" she yelled. All I could think of was which one of them bamma-ass niggas told this girl my name was K-man. I hated that shit. See, niggas at school still associated K-man to me being a boy, and like I said, things had changed and now I was a man.

I turned around to get a good look at her. I knew she was trying to get up with me because my man Bricks told me earlier that day. Come to think of it, he was probably the one who told her to call me K-man. Punk-ass nigga.

I turned around real smooth and said, "What up, shawty?"

"Did Bricks give you my message yesterday?" she asked

21

while sucking on a lollipop.

"Yeah he did. I figured he was lying and shit because I know you dealing with Scarface."

She started laughing and I knew she was getting ready to cut his ass quicker than I could give the word.

"He all right, but I'm trying to see what's up with you."

I signaled for Bricks and the rest of them niggas to go ahead to Checkers. They were playing me too close with their backpacks on and shit. I didn't need a band of brothers following me while I was talking to a girl.

When they were out of ear shot I said, "Listen, I'ma be straight up, I'm feeling you, but if you feelin' me, you gonna have to get rid of Romeo."

"If you can promise me that you won't play games, he can be gone by yesterday."

I smiled and the rest was history. Me and Lakeisha been kickin' it and fuckin' ever since. She was *the* baddest bitch in school and I constantly had to fight over her. It wouldn't be so bad if she kept her mouth closed. She drew too much attention and sometimes I wasn't feelin' that shit.

I mean, did she have to say something if shawty's shoes is banged out everyday? Couldn't she let the girl slide one time? Damn! But that was her thing, clownin' other chicks who ain't have shit. Whenever a chick would come to school with some Bo Bos on, she and her friends would be cracking jokes and shit, up against the lockers. She could do that because her mother was a stripper at Club 55 and kept her in all the finest shit.

I didn't care nothing about her cracking jokes, but if she said something to the wrong chick, she'd be sure to tell her boyfriend and you can guess the rest. Later on I'd have some clown-ass nigga trying to put Lakeisha in her place, so I had to put him in his. Her mouth was the only problem I had with her and that was within her control, not mine.

A Hustler's Son

The other problem I had was all mine, honestly. Charles was still pissed about losing his girl to a Freshman. That nigga was a Senior. He was held back twice and was still crying over a girl. Whenever he saw me in the halls, he'd have something to say and I would, too. I didn't like to keep up too much shit because they'd call my mother and then she'd have to take off work to see about me. I didn't like putting that type of pressure on her, so I let some shit slide. But even she understood when a nigga had to defend himself. So if she was coming to the school, she knew it was the real deal. I wasn't getting' in trouble for dumb shit.

When Bricks and I reached the school, we made it just in time before the first bell rang. I gave him some dap, he went to his class and I went to mine. Usually I was five or 10 minutes late but lately I had been on time, but my teacher *still* wasn't giving out no cool points for that shit.

"Mr. Davis, I'm glad you could join us."

"Come on man, I ain't even late."

"My name is Mr. Alverez. How many times do I have to remind you, Mr. Davis, or do I have to remind Ms. Stayley?"

"Listen, you can remind me or my Moms all you want, like I said, I'm here on time, so get off my case."

I couldn't stand his punk ass. If he thought he was gonna punk me in my Sophomore year by threatening to tell my Moms, he had another thing coming. My girl was in the class and everything, what I look like saying, "Please don't tell my mommy?" Fuck him!

"Just go to your seat so we can get started on the math problems, Mr. Davis."

When I walked to my seat my baby was sitting at her desk, right behind mine, looking all sexy and shit. She had on this red dress I never saw before. Whenever she wore a dress, she'd open her legs so I could see her panties the moment I walked in class.

I could always tell when she was mad at me because dress or not, her legs would be closed shut.

Today she had them wide open and I could see her turquoise panties. I had to hurry up and sit down before I got all hard and shit. I leaned back a little so she could talk to me and I kept my head turned toward the class.

She sat up all long and straight. I could smell her apple breath from the candy she was eating.

"Hey baby," she said as she whispered in my ear.

Like I said, my desk was right in front of hers so talking to me was easy for her, but harder for me. If Mr. Alverez's punk ass wasn't looking at me, somebody else was. I had carried a lot of bitches to fuck with Lakeisha, and they were all in my class, and were still mad about it. They'd be the main ones telling Mr. Alverez I was too loud and then he'd call my Moms. I'd already put her on to his ass a long time ago, and she was ready for him.

"Damn girl! You had to wear the turquoise ones?" I said in a low voice.

"Yeah, I knew you'd like 'em. I'm still seeing you after school today, right?"

"You know it."

After the last class, I was out the door and waiting for Lakeisha in the hallway. My boys knew what time it was, so they didn't bother waiting on me like they usually did. When I saw Lakeisha hit the corner in that red dress, my dick got hard immediately.

"Hey baby. You ready?"

"Hell yeah. Let's get the fuck outta here," I said as we headed for the door.

"You know whatever you're going to do to her, I've already done."

When I turned around I saw Charles' whack ass standing behind us. He always hated on Fridays because he knew we'd be together all weekend, so approaching me in the hallway wasn't unusual. It was just getting boring.

"Is that why you're still crying like a bitch?"

By this time a crowd was surrounding us waiting for us to go at it. That's the only thing that changed my way of thinking, a crowd. I didn't like nobody trying to play me, especially in front of my girl. If we were alone, I may have said a few things and left because I could tell he was a punk, but since he insisted on saying shit in front of people, he was getting exactly what he deserved, *carried.*

"Kelsi, can we just leave? Don't pay any attention to him," she said as she grabbed my arm.

"You used to pay attention to me, Key. Plenty of attention."

"Damn nigga, it's over. I snatched her because she was never yours to began with. Why do you think it was so easy?" I laughed, trying to add insult to injury.

"You ain't snatch shit, I gave her to you."

"So if you gave her to me, why you being a damn Drama Queen all up in the hall and shit? Talkin' about you *gave her to me*. Nigga you comical."

When he didn't say anything, and all the laughs everybody made from my last comment stopped, I walked away, arm in arm with the one thing I knew he wanted, Lakeisha.

"I thought so," I said as I offered him my back, and walked out the door.

It didn't help that she was wearing this sexy-ass red dress that clung to her thick-ass titties. He was lusting over them and couldn't get nowhere near 'em because they belonged to me. Usually we would have went at it for at least three rounds but he let me off a little easier today.

Once we were outside Lakeisha said, "Baby, he's so stupid. I can't believe he's still tripping."

"Girl please, you have some mean-ass pussy. I'd probably be

hunting your ass down, too."

"No you wouldn't, boy. I have a feelin you'd cut my ass off real quick."

She was right. I ain't in the business of sweatin' no female, even if she was my girl.

"He feelin' you, that's all. You ain't feelin' him are you?" I asked, just for kicks. I knew she wasn't trippin' off his weak ass.

"No. Charles is so over. I don't know why he's still trippin' off of me. I don't understand."

"You sure you don't like the attention. I mean, he stay blowin' you up makin' you look real big at school."

"I don't like that dumb shit! Every week it's the same thing. He ain't got nothing on you, Kelsi," she said as stood on her toes to give me a kiss.

She was right, and we both knew it. Charles went wrong in so many ways. He tried to win her back by begging every fucking day, instead of letting her come to him. It was the weakest shit I've ever seen. To be a senior, Charles needed serious lessons but I didn't have time to teach him.

We were almost near The Woods when Charles pulled up next to us in his car. At first I couldn't tell it was him because the sun was in my face and Lakeisha had me all wrapped up into what she was *gonna* do to me, once we made it to my place.

I was about to take off my hoodie because it was September, and only cool in the mornings and at night. Once I got it off, the shit fell to the ground, and I bent down to pick it up, which gave Charles more opportunity to catch my ass slippin.

"So what you got to say now?!" Charles threatened as he jumped out of the car.

I was mad at myself for slipping and not watching my back. Niggas was always getting stuck up for stupid shit, and here I was, feenin' over pussy that I already had, and I allowed Romeo to catch me off guard. I pushed Lakeisha away from me because he ain't never approached me around my hood, and I knew if he did, he must have been 'bout it. The nigga was packin' heat, he had to be. He knew I had people and even if I didn't, the niggas around here ain't go for new faces unless you was a girl. Where was everybody now?

"Nigga what the fuck is your problem?" I laughed.

"You're my fucking problem. I'm not even tripping off that bitch no more!" he yelled as he pointed at her.

"I'm your problem? Oh, so what, you wanna fuck me now?" I joked, although I probably shouldn't have.

"Man, fuck that shit you saying. I'm here because you talk too much shit and I want Lakeisha to see what happens to babbling bitches."

"Listen, take that weak-ass 1990 300 ZX, and get the fuck from around my hood."

"You talk a lot of shit for a nigga that's kickin' rocks."

"Yeah but I'm kickin' rocks with your ex-girl. She ain't complaining, nigga."

When he lifted up his shirt and showed me his gun, my heart stopped for five seconds. I mean, I knew he had it, but I wasn't ready to see it. He kept his shirt up for a minute for me to take in what he had in store for me. He wanted the look of *fear* to stay on my face but I replaced it with *hate*.

"Baby, go home. I'll get up with you later."

"I can't leave you here, Kells." She started crying.

She lived in Palmer Park, which was about 20 minutes away, and used her friend's address in Kenilworth Towers to be zoned for Bladensburg High. I wanted her to catch the bus on the corner and go the fuck home.

"Lakeisha! Get the fuck outta here and go home! Now!" I yelled at her.

The next words he said made me want to choke the life out of him.

"Key, get in my car!"

"What?" she asked, as she was breathing harder and crying at the same time.

"I said, get in my car!"

"Man, Lakeisha ain't going nowhere with you. This is between me and you."

"Oh yeah? What the fuck you gonna do about it, nigga? You not Mr. Funny Man out here. I should put this barrel in your mouth right now." He was so close to me, I could feel his heart-beat.

He kept the edge of his shirt up so I could still see the weapon in his pants. He even tilted his head a little like he was saying, "Is there a problem?" That clown had watched *Boyz N the Hood* one too many times for me.

All I wanted was for Lakeisha to take off running because I knew if she got in his car, he would rape her. I could see this punk taking advantage of my girl. I was mad when I turned my head and saw her still standing there. I could be stronger if she weren't there. I wouldn't have to worry what would happen to her, or if she would get caught in crossfire.

"Keisha, get the fuck outta here!"

"Key, I said get in the FUCKING CAR!" he yelled as each word caused him to spit in my face.

"Man, my girl ain't goin' nowhere wit you!"

"Fuck you nigga!"

She wasn't listening to either of us.

I didn't care what he did. I couldn't see my baby getting into this nigga's car. I just couldn't! I didn't want him touching her soft thighs, sucking her breasts or kissing her lips ever again. I also hated myself even more for not wanting her if he did touch her. She was my girl and if he fucked her, as far as I was con-cerned, she'd be tainted. I know it was fucked up, so it was all the more reason for me to stop this bamma from putting her in his car.

I had to do something because Lakeisha wasn't moving. I know what I was thinking about doing next was just plain stupid; if I fucked up, I could get shot and so could she. But I had to do something so I decided to go for the heat.

I grabbed him by his shirt to get him off balance. When he stumbled, I stole him in his face. See, niggas ain't know how to go with the hands no more, so when I hit him, his eyes got wide as shit. I stole his ass again trying to close 'em shut. I knew he couldn't scrap, because most niggas couldn't. He was too busy hiding behind his gun that he wasn't expecting me to use my fists. Fighting straight up was the only thing my father taught me when he got out of jail. *Aim for his temples!* he used to tell me. He told me that if you hit somebody in their temples hard enough, you could make them unconscious. My fists connected with this nigga's nose, eyes and lips. Funny thing is, I don't even know if any of my blows made it to his temples.

He was down for a second, and again, I told Lakeisha to run.

"NO!" she cried. "I'm not fucking leaving you!"

"Bitch, get the fuck outta here," I said in between stomping the fuck out of that nigga's skull as he tried to get up. I had him up against the fence getting the best of him. Between the stomping and the kicking, I demolished my brand new butters. Shit! Because of this bamma I had to buy a new pair. Just for that, I stomped his ass again.

Lakeisha was still standing there, like a deer caught in headlights.

"Get the fuck out of here Lakeisha, before I fuck you up!" I told her.

"I'm not leaving you, muthafucka!" she cried with her face soaked in tears. "So you might as well do what you gotta do!"

"Do I look like I need your help?!" I asked as I stomped him with each word I spoke.

29

"Baby, I'm not leaving!"

Damn this girl is stubborn! I thought by calling her a bitch she would get mad and leave but I should have known that wouldn't work. That was the reason I chose Lakeisha. Outside of her body and her sex game, she was down for me FOR REAL, and I knew that. Even to this day, she proved it even more.

In between stomping Charles up against the fence my shirt got hooked onto one of the wires. I couldn't get it off. That was long enough for him to get up and point the gun to the back of my head. I stopped struggling to release myself and held my hands up as if he were P.G. County police. He slammed me against the fence with my back facing him.

He cocked the gun and said through clenched teeth, "If you move, I swear to God I'll pull this trigger."

I wasn't sure, but something told me after the beating I just gave him, he meant it. Before I could even think about it some more, he hit me in the head four times with the butt of the gun, and I fell to the ground. Flashes of light and colors flooded my eyes, but then I couldn't see anything because blood was gushing over them. It felt like warm streams of oil. I grabbed the fence and tried to pull myself up. I was trying to see where Lakeisha was. All I saw was the red dress I had fantasized about all day being forced into his car.

"Lakeisha! Lakeisha!"

I tried to run over to the car but my equilibrium was all fucked up and I fell over again. When I finally got up, they were gone. I leaned up against the fence, and wondered what was next.

In the Apartment
3:45 pm

Our apartment looked weird. After being held at gunpoint,

everything looks different, even the place you call home. I don't know if the blow that nigga dealt had me noid, or if I was changed more now than ever before, but for some reason, my senses were heightened. The only thing is now, it wouldn't do me any good. *Always watch your back, Kelsi,* is what she used to tell me. And what did I do? Get caught slippin'!

I ran through every room in the apartment to make sure he wasn't there, because truthfully, I ain't know what kind of dude I was dealing with. Prior to now he'd always been pansy-ass Charles. But after the stunt he just pulled, I ain't know who I was dealin' with. But I do know that he should've killed me. It's almost like I was given a second chance, but for what?

3:55 pm
"Bricks, I can't find her man! I don't know what I'm gonna do. Maybe I should go back out and try to find her."

"Naw, man! Stay right there. I'm gonna have my brother come pick you up in 15 minutes. We'll find her, Kells. I'm telling you right now, Bladensburg is too small for that nigga to get away with this shit."

"If he touched her I'll —"

"Look, we can't think about that shit right now. We gotta think about our next move. We'll get that bitch-ass nigga! Trust me."

"I hope so. That nigga is mine."

"No doubt," Bricks said. "We'll be there in a sec."

"Aight, man. Hurry up."

Bricks calmed me down because I felt in his voice that he was as mad as I was about what happened. He always said that nigga was a little extra as far as Keisha was concerned but we never thought he'd go this far. The moment I came in, I called Lakeisha repeatedly, hoping she would be at home, but knowing she wasn't. Maybe the knots I got on my head fucked up my frame of mind, because I knew she wouldn't be there. It didn't help that all of my calls went straight to her mother's voicemail where she played the entire song *Believe In Me*, by Raheem Davaughn.

Blood was all over my face and I was sure I would need stitches. There was no way in the world I could be here by the time my mother came home. She would lose it the moment she saw me, even though I was sure it looked worse than what it really was. *Damn!* I still couldn't believe this shit happened to me.

I walked into the bathroom to clean up some of the blood with a few dark washcloths. In case I didn't make it home in time to tell my mother what happened, I didn't want her seeing blood all over the white ones. She was too up on shit for me to throw them things away.

When the phone rang, I dropped everything to go answer it.

"Lakeisha?!"

"Naw, its Delonte. Did your Moms tell you I'm moving back in?"

"Yeah," I said all nonchalant and shit. Truth was, I didn't give a fuck. What he want me to do, stroke his nuts?

"Well, I'll be there in an hour."

See, now we had a problem. My girl was out there possibly getting raped, and this untrustworthy-ass nigga wanted me to wait around for him to maybe or maybe not bring his sweaty-ass socks to my crib? That wasn't happening.

"Yeah. I'll be here."

When I hung up I knew it was as likely for me to be here as it was for him to be around next week. You just never know.

I went to the bathroom and changed into the shirt I had on the edge of the tub. The bloody shirt looked like I was stabbed, shot and stomped. I stuffed the blood stained shirt in a plastic bag and put it under my mattress. I was going to throw it in the dumpster later when I had some time. I grabbed the box of Band-Aids from the medicine cabinet, and played doctor on the wound Charles caused. For real they weren't covering shit, but it helped stop the bleeding. A little. Five minutes later, Bricks and Melvin were calling me to come downstairs.

In Melvin's Truck
4:30 pm

I get it now – everything you go through in life builds you up to become a man. For those who don't go through shit, they will never have an idea of what it's like. If shit is easy all your life, you have a false impression of what the *real* world is like and you run the risk of getting set up. But when you're thrown out there like me, you're forced to do what the fuck you gotta do. I understood now more than ever. *What don't kill you makes your stronger, Kelsi.* I was starting to believe that more and more because plenty of niggas would have been terrified at what just happened, but to me, it all felt natural. I felt I was on the right path, even if it was the path of destruction.

I ran downstairs and jumped in his brother's black Durango. Melvin was cool as shit and was always down for anything. He'd gotten me and Bricks out of plenty of shit in our day, including the one night we got drunk and locked up after leaving Crossroads, a night club. Fucking with these broads, we didn't realize they got us for our wallets in the club. Instead of calling it a night, we decided to eat at IHOP and leave without paying. Melvin came all the way down from D.C. to get two drunk-ass bastards out of Upper Marlboro's holding cell that was about 40 minutes away from where we lived. That's the only time being a minor paid off, because Moms would have flipped if she had to come get me for stealin' pancakes and shit. Outside of Bricks, Melvin was the only nigga I really fucked with.

"Hey lil' nigga. I heard what happened. If we find that

nigga, I'm whoopin' his ass."

"Thanks Melvin, but that nigga's mine. If he put his hands on my girl, I'm killin' him. I just need you and Bricks to have my back in case he tries to slug me."

"A lil' nigga after my own heart."

"We think we saw the Z near Capital Plaza on the way coming to get you, so we're going back there now," Bricks said.

"For real?" I asked, wondering why they just didn't go there and get her. I mean what if he got away? I would have been real salty about that shit.

"Yeah, it looked like his old-ass car but it was just parked. I figured you live right around the corner so even if he drove up the street, we could still catch up with his ass," Bricks said.

"You right. As long as we find him before he rolls out, I'm good."

"Where his punk ass live anyway?" Melvin asked.

"He live in Landover. Somewhere near Landover train station."

"Well what the fuck is he doing going to Bladensburg?" Melvin asked.

"Exactly!" I said. "He's almost as old as you and still in high school. How old are you anyway, Melvin? 54?" I joked trying to make myself laugh when wasn't shit funny.

"Naw lil' nigga, I'm 35 and old enough to be your Pappy." He laughed.

When he said that I didn't want to admit it, but in a way I wished he were. My father wasn't about shit. He came by when he got ready, and dropped me off some cash every now and again. I cared more about the million dollar insurance policy he bragged on having than I did about him.

When we pulled up in the Capital Plaza's parking lot, I spotted that nigga's car right away. Everything in me wanted to tell Melvin to run his shit over but I had to think clearly because of

Lakeisha. If I reacted too quickly she could be in more danger. I wish she would have listened to me and gotten on that fuckin' bus!

"There's his car. Park right there, next to the McDonald's," I whispered as if Charles could hear me.

"Yeah, I see his ass. I'm gonna park behind it so we can run up on him," Melvin said.

When I got out of the truck, I walked toward his car. I tried to stay out of sight because I didn't want him spotting me before I knocked the shit out of his ass. Plus, I didn't want him pulling off if Lakeisha were still in the car.

Melvin didn't follow me and Bricks because he went toward his trunk. When I looked to my left, I saw Bricks creeping real low like he was in a scene from *Menace II Society*. It was weird to watch because at 5'9" and 240 pounds, Bricks wasn't a small dude. I seen that black-ass muthafucka crush many niggas in his day.

When I turned around, I saw Melvin and more importantly, what he had in his hand. I was ready for war now that I knew he was packing. I picked up a big-ass rock in the parking lot and put it in my pocket.

"What you doin' with that shit, nigga? Stoning him to death?" Bricks asked.

"Fuck you, nigga."

When we reached the car, I was hot when I ain't see Lakeisha in the passenger seat. Bricks had planned on snatching her out of the car while I handled my business with Charles, but now I didn't know where my baby was. It made me mad as hell to see Charles' pansy ass laughin' on his cell phone, lookin' like a bitch. When he looked up and saw me at his window, he was shook. I took the rock I had in my pocket and crushed his window. Glass went everywhere but I wasn't worried about getting cut. I'd seen enough blood today to be immune to any pain or fear.

I grabbed him by the shirt and was trying to pull him through the broken window. He was fighting me but I kept the hold I had on him. He was almost as tall as me, so pulling him out wasn't working. Bricks came to my side of the window and together, we were ripping his shirt to shreds trying to get his ass out the window, but it wasn't working. When we realized it was dumb to pull his clown ass through the window, I decided to open the door.

"Hold up, Bricks," I said, out of breath. "Don't let his ass move."

Melvin was right behind us making sure Charles didn't get away and no one would approach us.

I reached in the window, unlocked the door, and pulled him out. Bricks turned his ass around and threw him up against the car. He wanted to make sure he didn't have the gun he used to bludgeon my face earlier. I was sure he didn't because P.G. County Police would have locked his ass up with a quickness, and he knew I was looking for his ass. He'd be dumb as shit to have a gun on him now.

"He's clean," Bricks said like he was a cop.

"Where the fuck is Lakeisha?"

"She ain't here, nigga!"

I looked in his eyes and all I saw was fear and I loved it. I wondered if I looked like he did now when he approached me earlier with that piece.

"I see that, bitch! So where the fuck is she?!" I asked as I walked up closer to him.

With Melvin on my left and Bricks on my right, we stood in front of him like we were P.G. County's finest.

"Man, uh, get the fuck out my face. I said she ain't here. What the fuck you want me to say? Huh?! "

"Is this nigga tryna break?" I said as if I were talking to my boys.

Yeah, this nigga was trying to break bad and I was tired of talking to him. I figured he'd done something to Keisha, and there was no reason he should even be existing.

I was just getting ready to use the blade I carried in my pocket when I saw Melvin's 6'3", 300 pound frame walk toward him. Charles' entire expression changed. The fear I provoked in him earlier had worn off and had been replaced with the fear he had for Melvin.

There we were in the middle of the parking lot of Capital Plaza, and I could have sworn that nigga was on the verge of crying.

"Lil' nigga, you got five seconds to tell me where my man's girl is."

"She ain't here. Uh, her friend saw us driving down the street and she went with her. I wasn't gonna do shit to her, I just wanted to talk to her."

"Dude, she's not your girl, so what the fuck you gotta talk to her about?" Melvin asked with the gun visibly showing in the front of his jeans.

I knew this was my business but I loved seeing Melvin getting in that nigga's shit.

"Uh, I, uh wanted to talk to her about us. Did he tell you she used to be my girl?!"

"Dude, you sound like a bitch! You's a sucka for love ass nigga for real!" Bricks laughed.

"I don't care what you think. Like I said before, I wanted to talk to her about us!" Charles said.

"You wanted to talk to her about us. They told me you was a bitch but I had no idea," Melvin said as he pulled out a gun. "Well since you like to hit folks with weapons, I'm going to return the favor. And if you move, *if you move,* I'll be using the other end of this gun. You feel me lil' nigga?"

"Pleaseee ... don't," Charles begged.

"M, let me handle this."

"You got it, Kells," Melvin said as he handed me the piece.

It was the first time I ever held a weapon in my hands outside of a blade I carried to school sometimes. I'd seen 'em all the time but niggas don't like you touchin' their shit. For a minute, I looked at it and admired its power. I could do anything I wanted with it between my fingers. I looked down at the gun, and held it in a position that commanded authority. Charles' expression changed once again, but this time I didn't need Melvin or anybody else to make him fear me. For that one second, to him, I was God.

"I'm gonna ask you one more time," I said as I cocked the gun. "Where the fuck is my girl?"

Melvin and Bricks looked around to make sure no one was watching in case I shot this muthafucka right where he stood. I don't even know how I knew how to cock the gun, maybe from playing video games or maybe it was instinct. It could have been the thought of him on top of my girl, and her begging him to stop. It could have been him going in and out of her and her screaming for me to help, even though I wasn't near, or it could have been pure unadulterated hate.

I was so mad now, I was five seconds from blowing his head off. My hand was shaking, my finger and the trigger were about to become one. Charles was sweating bullets as he stood up against his car. Melvin took two steps next to me and said, "Be sure. Just be sure."

I knew what that meant, and I *was* sure. I was sure I wanted to kill him but I *wasn't* sure if he was telling the truth. What if she was OK and I'd gone too far? I didn't want my Moms coming to see me in the oranges behind bars. She had enough problems dealin' with these niggas in her life. I ain't want to add to her burdens. The thing is, because I thought of how she would feel if I took his life, I spared his and he ain't even know it. Didn't even have a clue! But this bitch-ass nigga wouldn't be getting off so easy either.

I took the Glock and changed the position from that of authority, to that of a ruthless object that I used to come across his face, like he did mine. Once down, Bricks started stomping him liked he'd kidnapped his girl. Normally, I handled business on my own, but he deserved what he was getting, he deserved it all. I'd be mad as hell later if I found out he actually raped Lakeisha and I let him get away unscathed and I was mad at how my mother would feel the moment she saw my face. So for five more minutes, we punished his ass in the middle of the parking lot, until we were tired.

When we felt he received the proper beating, Melvin reminded him to stay the fuck away from me and Lakeisha on Monday at school, and he said that he would. After everything we did today, I knew I'd be seeing him again and it wouldn't be in passing.

Back at the Apartment
6:15 pm

When I made it back to the apartment, Valentino was sitting in the parking lot, with his shit in his Escalade, ready to move back in. I knew that nigga was a pusher and that kinda irritated me too because I ain't want my Moms involved in no bullshit. So what I pushed weed, but that nigga pushed coke and I ain't like him. Truthfully, everything that cat did irritated me.

"Your boy's here," Bricks said as we all looked out the window.

"I see his punk ass." I glared at him through the window.

"Your Moms got his ass open. She be straight playin' his ass though. How you put a nigga out every week?" He laughed.

"What I don't understand is why he keep comin' around this

muthafucka!" I added as we observed his ass in his truck.

I could have gotten out right away, but I wanted to see how anxious he was. And there he was, moving back and forth, like he was gonna die if he didn't get in the apartment right now. He was mad as shit at me. Like she was in the apartment waiting for him and he was going to melt if he didn't see her in the next five minutes. This nigga's a pussy for real!

"Well I'm out. I made this nigga suffer long enough," I told them.

"Later. Let me know if you see any spottings," Bricks said. "We ain't got no problem finishing that nigga off."

"No doubt." I told him. "Thanks, Melvin."

"You got it, man. Later."

When I jumped out of Melvin's truck, I told them I'd get up with them later. Delonte got out of his truck and followed me like some love-sick puppy.

"Where you been? I told you I was coming. I've been waiting out here all day," he said as he followed me to the apartment door. "And why was you taking so long getting out of the truck when you knew I was waiting out here?"

"Come on man, how you gonna be out here all day when you just called two hours ago?"

"You know what I mean."

"Naw I don't," I said as I made my way to the apartment and opened the door.

Delonte followed behind me, put the big-ass trash bag down he was carrying, and sat next to me on the couch, eyeballing my face.

"Do you have to sit on the same couch with me? We ain't in love!"

"I'm trying to get a good look at your face."

"Well don't you have to be sitting across from me to do that?"

"You know your mother is gonna be mad as hell, right? What the fuck happened to you, youngin'? You got jumped or something?"

"Naw, I don't get jumped and I don't have time to talk to you about it anyway."

"Why not, lil' nigga? What you got to do that's so important?"

"Why the fuck you worried about it?" I asked.

He was askin' a million questions and all I wanted to do was call my girl. I needed him out of my space and I could tell he wanted to be in my business.

"Because your mother is my woman and when she's not here, you're my responsibility, *Kells*."

Only my friends called me Kells, and I knew he knew that. That ain't do nothin' but piss me off even more.

"Yeah well, my Moms being your woman is some unfortunate-ass shit that ain't got nothin' to do with me."

"Watch it, youngin'."

"Don't you have some coke to sell?"

"You know what, lil' nigga," he said as he stood up.

See, this is what fuck I'm talkin' about. I was ready for this shit. Get mad, nigga. I jumped up and got right in his face. When you've been inducted into manhood, you can look an imposter in his face and know the difference. If he ain't a man, he'll fear you, and he feared me. His eyes looked for something in me that wasn't there. He was lookin' for a 15-year-old boy that I ditched along time ago. I hated him and needed an excuse to do something about it. I had plans to fuck him up and tell my Moms he started it. In my mind, she'd understand.

Bottom line was this, I had a lot of shit *still* on my chest, and I hadn't fully gotten it off yet. His face was the perfect canvas I needed to express my creativity. I was so close to him now, that if he would have breathed on me, I would have knocked his ass out.

"Fuck you, K!" he spat as he walked out of the door to get the rest of his shit.

"Yeah, that's what I thought." I grabbed the phone, walked to my bedroom and closed the door.

A Hustler's Son

I was so happy to be home I didn't know what to do. There was no way in hell I could have made it to my second job. Although I knew in the back of my mind I was excited about Delonte being back, I was also exhausted. When I got out of the cab I walked toward my apartment building and saw Delonte's truck. There's something about seeing those D.C. tags against that white truck that did something to me. The moment I saw it I thought, *Daddy's home.*

Before entering the building I noticed someone watching me walk in. He was wearing a black jacket with a hood and had a large scar on his face. I grabbed the knife in my pocket and again, flashbacks of my past entered my mind. *Please don't let me die like this, on the steps of the place that has been my safe haven for years,* I thought. The only thing that calmed me down was him saying, "Good Evening, Mrs. Stayley. Can you tell Kelsi that I said hello." See *they* would not have known me by that name. I nodded my head yes and walked into my building, but the knife remained clutched in my hand, just in case.

I went to the mailbox and pulled out the mail. I hated how the Pennysaver magazine always surrounded the *real* mail. I quickly thumbed through everything and still didn't see a child

43

support check from Lorenzo. *I can't stand his ass.* He don't ever pay on time.

I walked to the door and fumbled around for the key. It was then I remembered that I'd have to get Delonte a new set made. The moment I opened my door, I felt something was up. Kelsi wasn't in the living room waiting on me like he usually was, and Delonte was sitting on the couch tight-faced. He promised he'd have dinner waiting for me when I got home, but when I looked at the kitchen table, all I saw was a box of cold Domino's pizza.

"Hey baby, we gotta talk," he said the moment I walked through the door.

"Delonte, please don't start with me. I'm extremely tired and I want to come home to a peaceful night with both of the men I love," I said exasperated as I threw the mail on the table and kicked off my shoes.

"Well that's what I want to talk to you about. The other man you love."

Just then, Kelsi walked into the room with his head bandaged up. I ran over to him, dropped my purse on the floor, and my knees buckled because I was terrified by the thoughts that clouded my mind.

"Baby, what happened?!" I asked, reaching toward his head.

"Nothing, Ma. It's not as bad as it looks," Kelsi said, pulling away so I wouldn't touch his wound.

I immediately looked at Delonte. If he laid his hands on my baby, I'd kill him and he'd be out of that fucking door forever. No changing locks, no playing games and no questions asked!

"I didn't touch him. I was the one who took him to Prince George's Hospital to get stitches. He had to get 15 over his right eye." He knew what I was thinking and came quick with an explanation. I knew in my heart that he wasn't stupid enough to touch my child, but I still had to ask.

"15 stitches?! Are you serious?" I asked. "Baby, what happened?"

K-man was standing in front of me like I was making a big deal for nothing.

"K-man, did you hear me? What the fuck happened?"

"It was nothing, Ma. I was playing football at school and one of them niggas tackled me against the concrete."

"Let me get this straight," Delonte said. "Your face fell up against the concrete? The last time I checked, there wasn't any concrete on a football field, man."

"That's cuz you play with pussies!"

"Hey! Watch your mouth, K-man! You're still a child. What has gotten into you?" I asked as I grabbed his arm. "Don't get smacked! You hear me?!"

Kelsi was seriously scaring me more and more each day. His defiance was borderline disrespectful and I hated the idea of losing my sweet boy. We always had a close relationship, and with these men coming in and out of my life, Kelsi was all I had. We joked all the time about it being just me and him against the world and now, here he was, cussing in front of me like I was some whore.

"I'm sorry, Ma," he said as he placed both hands on my face. "I had a rough day and I didn't mean to disrespect you. Please forgive me. It will never happen again."

I looked at Kelsi and I remembered when he was born. My baby was so handsome. As he grew, his words and demeanor had changed him into a man. That realization was something I wasn't ready to accept, but I knew, in due time, I would have to. Still, something else was going on with him and it was killing me not to know. I needed to know and needed to know now! I decided to speak to him alone.

I picked my purse up off the floor and turned around to face Delonte.

"I'm gonna talk to Kelsi for a minute. I'll be back in a few."

45

"Yeah well, don't forget you have a man to tend to," he said as he thumbed through the channels with the remote control.

"Like you'll let her forget," Kelsi retorted defiantly.

"Come on baby, please stop doing this," I responded as I walked with Kelsi to his room.

He sat on his bed and put his face in his hands. With my housekeeping uniform still on from the Sheraton, I walked around and examined his room. Although we lived together, I never violated his space. I always knocked on his door before entering. I gave him the privacy I never got from my mother when she was alive. If she wanted something, she'd walk right in my room and I didn't want to do the same thing to Kelsi. So entering his room was always like the first time to me.

His room was one of the cleanest places in the house. Boxes were lined up against the wall with his shoes, and his hats were stacked neatly on the shelf in the closet. He was a neat freak and rearranged stuff a lot, so every time I did come in his room, there was always something new I'd notice.

Like now, I was looking at the pictures he had on his dresser. He had one of that little light-skinned girl, Lakeisha, stuck in his mirror, and every other picture was spread across his dresser except the three pictures he had framed of me. The last time I came into his room he only had one framed, and now there were two more. It felt good to know that my baby still loved me, even though he was growing up.

"Kelsi, what's going on?" I asked as I sat next to him and put my hands in my lap.

"I can't stand Delonte, Ma. I don't like how he treats you because I think you can do better," he said as he looked at me.

"OK, you want to start there?"

"Yes, Ma. Why do you keep dealing with that dude even after you found out he was messin' with his cousin?"

"Don't talk about stuff you don't know about, Kelsi."

"Ma, Kenosha came over here right after you put him out, hollering about she wanted to talk to you about what you *thought* you saw. She starts telling me she wasn't *really* kissin' him in the car. I knew right then what was up."

"How come you ain't tell me that girl came by my house?"

"Come on, Ma, I know you ain't tryna talk to that girl. She a chickenhead. Anyway, you're beautiful and too good for that nigga! I have to beat my friends down now for looking at you the wrong way. They swear you're my sister instead of my mother."

"For real?" I said, smiling hard.

"Ma!"

Damn, I can't even play with him in certain ways no more. Everything about him was the same but different. He was *still* my son, and he was *still* my responsibility but he was *now* a man. I felt the love he had for me as strong as I felt the hate he had for Delonte.

"I'm just playing, baby. I respect what you're saying because I know you're serious. Don't worry about Delonte because he's my problem and as wrong as he may be, I love him. You have to let me live my life like I let you live yours."

"I'll kill him, Ma. I swear to God I'd kill anybody who tries to hurt you." A lot of conviction was in his voice as he looked me dead in my eyes as if I were Delonte himself.

Instead of telling him not to ever say that again, I took comfort in knowing that someone cared enough about me to take another life. To me, it was the ultimate love and sacrifice. Some people might say it was sick, but all my life I wanted someone to love me and be willing to do anything for me. For the first time in my entire life, I was hearing those words from my son, and the effect it had on me felt better than anything any man could ever say.

"Baby, let me deal with Delonte and let me live my life.

OK?"

"OK, Ma," he said as he sat down next to me on the bed and continued, "but I'm serious about what I said."

"And so am I, now, what's really going on with your face?" I inquired as I placed my hand on his leg.

"I told you I bashed it playing football. Delonte's used to playin' on cushions and he don't know nothing 'bout no street ball. You know I tell you everything so why you worrying?"

"I know baby," I said as I fell into the one arm hug he gave me. "I just don't want that to ever change."

"It won't, Ma. You're all I have in this world. I'd die for you and die without you. Remember what you used to call me when I was little?"

"Boy, you still are little, ain't that much changed," I laughed and touched his face, and continued, "with the exception that you over six feet tall with a little chin hair and shit."

"For real, Ma. I'm dead serious. You used to call me your soldier and that's exactly what I am, *your* soldier. The only difference now is that I *can* protect you."

Kelsi's words sent chills up my spine because I could tell he was dead serious. Prior to having this talk, I only guessed that the little boy I nurtured and loved had changed, but now I was certain. He spoke with so much passion that I knew he meant every syllable in every word he said. I rested easier knowing that although I hated seeing his face in the condition it was in, I believed whatever was going on, he could handle it.

"I know, baby, but don't worry too much about Delonte. He isn't as bad as you think he is. He loves me in his own way. We just have to work through some shit." The more I spoke, the more I believed what I was saying.

Kelsi was quiet and I could tell he wasn't changing his mind about protecting me, or his opinion on how he felt about Delonte.

"Well, do you want me to warm you up some pizza?"

"No, I'm cool, Ma. I'll get something later."

"Well, I love you, baby." I reached in and gave him a hug, holding him a little longer, savoring the moment. I realized at that moment, and as a single mother, that I didn't do too bad of a job after all. Kelsi had never been in any major trouble, he was respectful and most of all he loved me.

When I stood up to leave, I turned around to ask him what made him frame the other pictures I'd given him over a year ago.

"Ma, why you ask me that?" he asked sounding like a 15-year-old boy for the first time since a few days ago.

"Because I want to know."

"Sometimes I don't get a chance to see you in the morning when I go to school. Before you got the second job, I was used to seeing you every day, you know? I framed the pictures to look at them before I leave out in the morning. It's like you're lookin' at me, and I know everything will be aight. Why you tryna make me all soft and stuff?"

"Kelsi, ain't nothing wrong with loving your mother," I said, laughing at his comment and blushing at his reasons.

"Ma, that's one thing I *do* know," he said in a serious tone.

His response caught me off guard because I don't know what I expected him to say, but it certainly wasn't that. He had me seriously thinking about ditching that second job to spend more time with him, because as much as he missed me, I missed him, too. The money I would lose from the second job wouldn't be a problem if Delonte and I could make it. It *really* wouldn't be a problem if Lorenzo paid his child support on time, but with K-man and Delonte going at it all the time, me and D staying together seemed even more impossible.

"I feel you and you're right, baby. I *am* looking over you and I *always* got your back."

"I know, Ma. I know. Hey Ma, before you leave –"

"Yes baby?"

"If someone's trying to take what's yours, or hurt what yours, do you have a right to defend it or protect it?"

I figured Kelsi was talking about me and the conversation we just had. Maybe he felt bad for saying he'd kill Delonte if he ever hurt me. In my heart I knew I should have set him straight. I should have said, "Kelsi, it's not right to say you'd kill somebody," but I didn't. In my heart, although it may have been wrong to others, I thought love that strong was selfless, and there was nothing wrong with it. I wasn't going to say anything to change his mind, because like he said, he was my soldier, and I wanted to keep it that way.

"Baby, you have a *right* to protect and defend anybody you love."

He looked up at me, smiled and said, "Thanks, Ma. I needed to hear that."

I was almost out of the door when I remembered I had two things to ask him.

"Kelsi, real quick, did you take Delonte's keys?"

"Naw, Ma. I know taking his keys won't stop him from getting in if you want him to. You the real lock and key." He laughed.

"I guess you right." I laughed. "Also, a friend of yours outside told me to tell you hello."

"How he look?" The smile he had immediately dissipated from his face.

"Umm, I don't know. He had a scar though."

"Thanks, Ma." I didn't know who he was, but I could tell *now* that he wasn't a friend.

"Good night, baby."

"Good night, Ma."

When I walked out his room, I was comforted by my relationship with Kelsi but strained by what was happening between Delonte and I. When I sat on the couch he was sitting down still tight-faced, playing with the remote control.

"What you watching?" I asked.

"I ain't watching nothing. The TV's watching me."

"Come on, Delonte, I need your support not your pressure."

"And I'm trying to give it to you but you're going to have to get Kelsi in check. I mean, who's the man in this house?"

I wasn't even going to begin to answer that question. Right now he was acting like a kid, and Kelsi had just proven to me that he was a man.

"Let's talk about this tomorrow, Delonte."

"Do you not see anything wrong with Kelsi and the way he's been acting?" he asked, turning his attention away from the TV and toward me.

It was now I who chose to use the TV as an escape. It's funny how a TV can be used to avoid issues and problems. Delonte and I had been using televisions to avoid problems throughout our entire relationship. As I watched Martin surprise Gina with a serenade from Brian McKnight, I seriously thought about Delonte's question. And the truth was, earlier I did see problems with the way Kelsi was acting, but now I understood him. And if he had a problem with Kelsi, he'd have to get over it.

"I think you should leave things alone," I told him, not taking my eyes off the TV.

"Whatever," he said as he walked toward our room. "And another thing, if a child tells you they'd kill somebody for you, you shouldn't let that shit slide. I don't take lightly to threats, Janet."

"And me either," I replied, feeling irritated by his comment. "Me either."

When he closed our bedroom door I was stuck, not because

he overheard what Kelsi said, but because I *still* didn't see anything wrong with it.

A Hustler's Son

When I walked through the doors of Landover Fire Department's community center, the place where they were having the party, I was a little noid. I knew I just butted a nigga with the end of a gun, and was pretty sure the beef was still on. Luckily for him, my girl was in one piece and hadn't been fucked with, at least that's what she told me.

The hall stunk and there were more sets of balls in there than there were bitches. Empty cups were thrown all over the floor, and I could tell right off the bat that the D.J. was weak. He was bumpin' that Stefani chick's song, *Holla Back Girl*. The song was *OK* if you didn't just barrel a nigga with a weapon, but I needed to hear something different, something for me – and that's when the D.J. played *Soul Survivor* by Young Jeezy. That's exactly what I needed! That's what was up.

"Kelsi, don't that broad look like Lakeisha?" Bricks asked.

I scanned the room to see who the fuck he was talking about. Nothing in there looked anything like my shawty.

"I know you not talking 'bout that chickenhead over there!"

"Whatever, man! Shawty looks just like Keisha and if you don't want her, shit, I'll get up on her," Bricks said as he walked away to lay down his weak-ass game.

There were only two or three muthafuckas on the floor and two of 'em were dudes. They were dancing all hard and shit. BAMMA NIGGAS! I'm not a dancing type, so even if I would hit the floor, I'd just stand behind the girl and press my shit up against her ass. Ain't no dancin' needed for that.

Really the only thing I was thinking about was Lakeisha, and if Charles did more than she told me he did. I had a feeling she'd lie to protect me instead of tell me the whole truth. She told me that when he kidnapped her and drove to the Capital Plaza lot to talk, he begged her to take him back, and of course she told his punk ass to get lost. Based on the time frame she told me, we must have just missed her before she left.

It just so happened that two of her friends noticed his whack-ass Z sitting in the lot, and approached the car. Lakeisha said later she didn't even know why they came to the car to begin with, because they knew she wasn't dealing with him no more, but I figured maybe one of them were feelin' him.

Anyway when Sparkle, one of the biggest freaks in school, approached his car, Lakeisha saw her chance to get away and asked if she could take her home. I'm glad he ain't see the cracked headlight of her old-ass Lexus and roll out. That shit's been broke since the dude she was runnin' bought it for her and she was too lazy to get it fixed. Since they all lived in Palmer Park, Sparkle agreed to take her home. I guess he got scared and let her go, because he couldn't hold everybody at gunpoint just to profess his love to my girl. The more I thought about it, if that nigga was really 'bout it like he thought he was, he woulda done it anyway.

That much I believed – Keisha not wanting him was why all this shit was happening. She even tried to say that everything was her fault but the way that girl was down for me, I wouldn't give a fuck how many niggas were after me, I would still be by her side. As long as she didn't lie to me, I'd be by her side. It wasn't because I was pussy-whooped or no shit like that, it was because I was sure that outside of Bricks, Melvin and my Moms, if some shit went down, she'd be right beside me, strapped up and ready for war. She'd already proven it.

"Man, these broads in here weak as shit," Bricks said as he walked up to me, sippin' on a drink.

"So what happened with the girl? She carried you?" I laughed.

"Yeah, OK," he responded.

"I thought you said mad bitches was gonna be here, man. Ain't nothing in here but some skeezas. I could have stayed at home with my girl."

"Why didn't you, nigga?"

"Cuz I wanted to see these fine-ass bitches you were yappin' about all week."

Truth was, I wasn't trippin' off none of them hoes in there. I was there because Bricks helped me punish a nigga on Friday, and I ain't want him catching the heat from it, if Charles happened to make an appearance tonight. See, I knew Charles was a punk and that Bricks could handle his own. The only thing that had me skeptical was that Charles wasn't thinking rationally. There was nothing more dangerous than a nigga who was in love and still trippin' off a girl he ain't have no more.

Nobody could totally blame Charles for tripping because Lakeisha was top flight. She didn't have a scar on her body and she gave head like it was going out of style. She wasn't one of them girls you had to beg to suck your dick by placing a 50 dollar bill on top of it. When she fucked, it was because she wanted to. Although I knew I wasn't her first, her pussy was tight and wet every time I hit it.

The more I thought about Lakeisha, the more I was ready to leave. My plan was to occasionally remind Bricks how weak this joint was without going overboard and sounding like a bitch.

"Man, this shit is whack," Bricks said. "We can leave in a few."

Good! I was so glad he said it before I had to. Bricks had Melvin's truck and Lakeisha was waiting for me at my house. Even though we were only 15, and turning 16 in a few months, Melvin ain't mind him using the truck if we were going right around the corner. We had fake IDs and everything, so if we got pulled over, we'd appear legit.

Bricks getting a ride was the only way I'd go to the party. Calling a cab around here took forever. That was one of the good things about staying at my father's place in Baltimore county. I could catch a hack anytime of day or night; but in Landover, if you jumped in somebody's car outside of a cab, you'd be lucky to leave with your life, let alone what's in your pockets.

As if I weren't already ready to roll, some dude bumped into this cat on the dance floor, and he was mad about it. They were dancing like two idiots, so it was just a matter of time before they knocked each other out. Two bitches! Yep, it was time for me to get the fuck out of here, so I could get up in Lakeisha.

I was also still thinking about my Moms and the conversation we had. I could tell she was worried about me and after our little talk, the only thing I realized was that I really couldn't stand that Delonte cat. I didn't like the way he talked to her, I didn't like him playing daddy, and lately, he had become too concerned with what the fuck *I* was doing. He had some nerve considering he had a lot of shit of his own to deal with.

For one thing, he hot boxed and told her I was pushing weed around the apartment complex last year. He got all swole up when he caught me, I think he wanted her to throw me out. That shit was hilarious because I knew my Moms would never do that shit. He just wanted me out the way so I couldn't see how he be treating her. What he didn't know was, if I left, I'd be even more dangerous. In a way it was good for him that I was still living there because the farther I got from my Moms, the more overprotective I'd get. My mother and I had a connection that got tighter the farther we got away from each other. I wasn't going to forget about her if I couldn't see her. All I'd do was think about her more.

"Kelsi, you got anything on you?" It was this dude I served sometimes in The Woods. "And what happened to your face, man?"

"I ran into your mother's fat ass, and NO, I ain't got shit. Why you sweatin' me at the Fire Department anyway?"

"Cuz I need somethin' tonight!"

"Nigga, get the fuck outta my face," I responded, trying to brush him off.

"Please, man."

"Why you feenin' ova green?" I asked him.

"My girl want it."

"Naw nigga, I'm out. Ask Bricks or somethin'," I said, tryin' to get the tick off my dick.

"All right, man."

Stupid nigga. Me and Bricks pushed together for Skully. Our first weight was moved faster than we got it. We wasn't fuckin' with coke, we were pushin' weed, and at the time, nobody else in the hood was really dealing with that. In The Woods, it was all about the crack. I ain't have no intentions of dealing forever, so when Delonte caught me, I asked him not to tell Moms, but this bitch went and did it anyway. That's where her second job came in. She thought I was doing it for extra cash but that wasn't the case. I was doing it for us. I didn't tell my Moms the reason because it wouldn't make a difference to her. I knew she ain't want me pushin', *period*.

It made a difference to that Chauncy-ass dude Delonte,

that's why he told her. He ain't like the idea of running into me selling in Autumn Woods, because that's were he pushed. He had been selling caine in the apartment complex for years. The only reason I didn't get too upset was because he was pushin' weight *way* before we moved over there five years ago, but with him hurting my Moms and staying in my business, we were starting to have some real issues. Plus, snitches get stitches, and it was time he got his.

"Kells, I'ma run to the bathroom real quick."

"You ain't got to make no announcements man. Just go!"

"Fuck you, nigga!" He laughed and grabbed his dick.

Clown-ass nigga. He knew he ain't have no business telling me he was going to the bathroom. That nigga had one too many drinks, and now he was lunchin'.

When I looked at my watch I noticed it was 10 o'clock and Moms wouldn't be home for another three hours. My girl was there *alone* with Delonte and while I didn't trust him, I trusted her. My Moms was cool with her chillin' at the crib when I wasn't there. That's another reason we had such a close relationship – she ain't trip off bullshit. When I hear about some of the shit my boys have to go through with their parents, it's no wonder they stay in the streets. Although I'm elbow to elbow with them, I'm in the street because I love my Moms, *not* because I hate her.

"I'm ready Kells, let's roll man," Bricks said when he came back from the can.

"I'm ready when you are," I said trying to act like I wasn't rushin' to dig Lakeisha's back out.

When we walked outside I felt something was up the moment my Timbs hit the concrete. The air was thick and it felt weird. *Watch your back, Kelsi,* she told me. I was caught slipping yesterday but I wouldn't be caught today. My Moms was a vet to violence because she'd been robbed twice and always warned me to beware of my surroundings. I knew she wasn't talking so much about the shit you could see as she was about the shit you couldn't.

"Hold fast, Bricks, something ain't right."

"What you mean, man?" he asked, looking around him.

"I don't know, I just have a feeling."

We both looked around and didn't see anything. I scanned quickly through the parked cars and alongside them and still saw nothing. A few cars whisked down Landover Road, which was always busy at night, but nobody was moving in our direction.

"Well whatever's going on, let's not stand in the parking lot like a couple of bitches waiting to be fucked. Let's get out of here," Bricks commanded.

"You right," I said, realizing standing there was only making us look stupid.

In the Truck
10:15 pm

When we jumped in the truck, I checked in the rearview mirror to be sure he wasn't following us. I knew his car window was gone and was pretty sure he hadn't fixed it yet, so chances were he wouldn't be driving it.

"Kells, you still thinking about that nigga, ain't you?" Bricks asked, after seeing me checking out my surroundings.

"That's all I'm thinking about, man. It's fucking me up cuz I don't see but one kind of ending to this story. It's just a matter of who ends it first."

"Look, that nigga know we not playin', and my brother all prepared to come back through if he comes back again," Bricks reassured as he approached my apartment complex.

Fight your own battles, Kelsi. You not a man until you fight your own battles.

"I appreciate that man, but ya'll can't be everywhere all the time. Pretty soon me and that nigga gonna come face to face, alone. And there's nothing I can do but be ready. I have to fight my own battles."

When the words left my mouth, I realized how serious shit really was, and all over a girl. If I had to go down, I always imagined dying for slinging in the hood, but not like this. When did my life change? Last week I was slinging in the hood and now I'm watching my back and fighting for my life.

"I hear you man, but there's more than one soldier in the battlefield. Remember that," Bricks said.

"Aight man." I laughed as I gave him dap. "I'm out."

When I got out, I was careful because my instincts were always on point. And although I didn't see him at the firehouse, something told me something was up, plus the nigga did pop up at my house, talking to my Moms and shit. Even if he didn't show up tonight, I was gonna have to fuck him up on sheer principles alone when I saw him.

Even though wasn't shit happening in Landover, now I was in my parking lot so anything could happen. It was dark and there weren't a lot of lights out there. Girls got raped all the time because of that shit, that's why every night I'd wait up until my Moms came home from work. I used to wait outside for her but she'd tell me, *How good do you think I'll be if someone hurt you? Wait for me in the house, Kelsi.*

I decided not to run but I wasn't bullshitting either. I took quick, big steps toward my building and was almost there when he came out of the bushes.

"Kelsi, don't even think about going in that apartment, man." He was calm and his voice didn't shake. Tonight was the night and I knew it.

With two deep breaths, I turned around to face my predator. My heart was pumping so much blood that I could feel it in my ears. Whatever was going down would be final. We both knew that unless somebody went down for good, I couldn't keep watching my back and he wouldn't be able to watch his. See, he had violated me too much by poppin' up over my house, so this was it. He didn't have any respect for me, so I didn't have any respect for his life.

"What you doing at my apartment, man? Didn't you get enough yesterday? And what the fuck you doin' sayin' shit to my Moms?!"

Charles stepped up and looked at me. For the first time I saw a man, and not someone who was willing to go the limit. I knew he was willing to kill me, just as much as I was willing to kill him, if I had to.

"Where's Key, man? I know she here, so go in the house and tell her to come out." He stared at me and nodded his head toward my apartment.

"Charles, Lakeisha doesn't want you, man. You can't keep poppin' up like Batman thinking that shit will work. She's my girl!"

"She wanted me before you came in the picture, Kells," he said as he walked closer to me. "I figured if you weren't in the picture no more, maybe she'd want me again." He walked over to me with his hands in the pockets of his sweatshirt.

He wasn't looking at me, he was looking through me, as if he were either drunk or high. I figured he did whatever he had to do to pump himself up to kill me. I ain't need shit but the hate runnin' through my veins.

I reached into my pocket and grabbed the pocket knife because I wanted to be ready. *You'll come to a point in life when it's survival of the fittest, be ready, baby,* she told me. I was ready. I took a few deep breaths and was preparing myself for the ultimate crime – murder.

"Charles –"

And that's when I heard it.

His hands were still in his pockets but I heard a familiar sound. It was the same sound I heard yesterday when the barrel of his gun was pointed to my head. *Click!* With all my strength, and while his hands were still in his pockets, I lunged at him before he could pull that bitch out.

Any other Saturday night there would be people walking in and out of the complex but tonight, nothing. Maybe it was fear of not wanting to see anything or get involved. Either way, I knew I had to kill this muthafucka. Maybe it was best nobody was around anyway, they'd get in my way and delay the process. May as well get this over with now.

We were rolling around like two niggas fighting for their lives, and we were. I was trying to gain control, but I also was trying to prevent him from getting a good grip on the gun. He stole me in my face and I stole him back. Hitting me was the least he could do and to be honest, I ain't feel shit.

Somehow he managed to pin me down and get on top of me, and there it was, the one thing I wasn't trying to see any time soon. I don't know if I hated the gun or the man more. For the first time in my life I was *really* scared because I knew the barrel pointed in my face had a bullet with my name written all over it.

"After I kill you, it won't be no problem getting my Key back, will it?" He was sweating and laughing like he'd lost his mind for real. I ain't say shit. He had the upper hand and I wasn't trying to hold it while he pulled the trigger. *Never let 'em see you sweat,* I heard her say, and I was trying not to. I swear to God I was. Still, this muthafucka was on top of me, and then he whispered in my ear, "Everybody has to die sooner or later, Kells." And it was true. As crazy as this muthafucka was, at this moment, what he was saying was true.

And suddenly I didn't give a fuck anymore. If he was gonna

pull the trigger, I wanted him to do it and get it over with. I was gonna leave in peace because I knew my Moms knew how much I loved her, and so did Lakeisha. I was ready to die even if it wasn't my time.

"Do what the fuck you gotta do," I told him as I looked him dead in his eyes. "You act like you scared to pull the trigger. Do it, bitch-ass nigga!"

He cocked the gun. I closed my eyes. He pulled the trigger. *Click.* If I were dead, it sure didn't feel like it. I wasn't in pain and to me it looked like I was still on the ground with this nigga *still* on top of me. I opened my eyes and he was still there, only now he was laughing like he was delirious.

"You one lucky nigga, but the next time you *won't* be," he said in a menacing tone.

The way I saw it, I had given up too easily on life. I was prepared to die by the hands of a sucker, and that couldn't happen. The gun being jammed was my queue to claim my life and take his.

Where was the knife? But, what was a knife going to do when this nigga had a gun? Anyway, I lost it when we first started going at it. I needed to buy more time before he pulled the trigger again because I knew next time, I wouldn't be so lucky.

"Hey Kelsi, before I kill you, did you smell my dick on Keisha's breath? She gives a hell of a blow job. I see you taught her a few tricks, too." Charles grabbed his dick through his pants and cupped himself with one hand, while still holding the gun tightly with the other.

There was no way this nigga was living after that shit. I had to kill him. I didn't even want to think about it being true although I knew it was a possibility.

"You got anything you want me to tell your mother after I kill you?" I asked in a low voice.

"What you say, nigga?" Charles licked his lips and held the

gun to my face again.

"I said, you got anything you want me to tell that *bitch* when I kill you?"

"And how do you propose to do that, bitch?"

"Like this."

While this nigga was straddling me like a bitch, I managed to locate the knife and I went across his face. *Slash!* Now this muthafucka had twin scars. He immediately lost control of the gun due to me catching him off guard. When he got off me, I jumped on him and stabbed him multiple times in the chest and back. He had on some jeans and a blue shirt which were now drenched in thick crimson-colored blood. He tried to scream but I went across his throat. *Take that!* I wanted him speechless. I took everything out on Charles, from the shit he did to me at school, to Delonte putting my mom through bullshit, to my father not being around. He personally became responsible for *everything* in my life.

I stabbed him so many times, that although I was stabbing his body, some of my jabs went straight to the ground.

When I got up I was covered in blood. His blood. I tore off his shirt and pants, and slid his body to the dumpster where the parking lot light had been broken for over a year. With all of the strength I had left, I lifted his limp body and threw it in the dumpster. I balled up his clothes and took off my shirts. It was cold outside but I was warmed by my own adrenaline and body heat.

I wiped off his gun and put it in my pocket. I don't know why I took it. Maybe it was a souvenir for taking his life. As crazy as I looked, I realized I still had to go home, covered in Charles' blood. Facing my girl and Delonte were the least of my worries, after all, I had just committed murder.

Kelsi
Chapter 5
September 17
Saturday, 10:45 pm

You did what the fuck you had to do, Kelsi. It was either that nigga or you, and guess what, it was him. I knew if ever there was a reason for murder, tonight was it. Charles would have been showin' up at my house until I put him out of his misery. It's bad enough my Moms lived here, I don't know what I'd do if she got caught up in all this shit. And then that bamma had the nerve to speak to my Moms. He crossed the line.

Walking through the hallway smelled different tonight. My senses were heightened because I was in another zone. I could smell everything including my neighbor's food, perfume, the detergent in the laundry room downstairs and now the ever-lingering scent of blood. Once again my senses were heightened and I was aware of everything going on inside of me and around me.

I dug in my pocket and grabbed the keys that were wrapped around the barrel of the gun. I got them loose and opened the door. The first thing I saw damn near drove me to murder all over again – Delonte and Lakeisha, sitting on the couch, watching TV together … laughing.

"I thought I told you to stay in my room, Lakeisha!" I yelled without even saying hello.

65

It was silent with the exception of the door closing behind me and my keys hitting the table.

"Did you hear what I said to you? I thought I told you to stay in my fucking room!"

It took me a second to remember I was covered in blood. That explained why the two of them sat stuck on the couch, staring at me. Delonte cut the TV off and stood up. He didn't walk over to me, he knew better.

"Baby!! What happened to you? What happened to your face?!" she screamed as she ran toward me, almost tripping over Delonte's feet.

I wasn't in the mood for her questions and I wasn't in the mood for her shit. I told her ass not to leave my room unless she wanted something to eat or drink, and there she was, sitting on the couch, looking at TV with the only other enemy I had *alive*.

"Are you OK, man?" Delonte asked.

I ignored him like he wasn't even in the room.

"Lakeisha, why are you in here? I don't want you around this muthafucka when I'm not home!" With each word, I raised my voice louder. I wanted her to understand I wasn't playing and I wanted him to hear *every* word I said. *Say something to me, muthafucka. Please.* He didn't. He saw murder in my eyes and I knew it. I stared at him longer so he could see it up close and personal. Without sayin' shit, I gave him a glimpse of what I'd do to him. He saw it, but only because I allowed him to.

I pushed Lakeisha toward the room, closed my door and reached underneath the mattress to grab the bag that held the bloody shirt I wore yesterday. I put the new blood-drenched clothes in the bag, and pushed it underneath the bed. I sat next to her on my bed and she moved away from me a little.

I took two deep breaths and tried to calm down. My Moms always told me before reacting, take two breaths. Although I always did it, it only gave me the energy to do what I was gonna do anyway. I wasn't trying to scare her but she made me mad. She should've stayed her hot ass in my room. My TV was the same size as the one in the living room, plus I had over 800 movies and 200 CDs. She couldn't be no more entertained out there than she could in here.

"I was bored." She was crying and breathing all hard and shit, but sympathy was something I didn't have a lot of because she didn't listen. "And what happened to you, Kelsi?"

"Baby, I'm OK. I just, I just had to handle some things tonight."

"What things?" she asked as she looked me over.

"Some *things,*" I emphasized in a low voice. "Don't worry about it though, I'll be OK."

Finally taking one good look at her, I smiled when I noticed she was wearing a pair of my boxers and a wifebeater. Her nipples were hard and her ass filled my boxers out so well, it was as if they were made for her. The smile was wiped away from my face when I noticed how sexy she looked. I didn't notice what she was wearing at first because I had just killed a man. Now, the thought of her sucking his dick, or riding him, filled my mind. Suddenly, a sense of calm took over my body as I realized how I reacted when I came in was justified. I didn't want my girl nowhere near that clown.

"Keisha, I love you, but I don't want you fuckin' with that dude." She put her head down. I lifted it back up. "Listen baby. *Don't* fuck with that dude." I wanted her to look in my eyes and know just how serious I was. I was on some whole different shit and we both knew it.

"OK Kelsi, but you're scaring me," she said as her chest moved along with her heavy breaths. "What's … what's … going on?"

"There's nothing to be scared of, baby. I wouldn't hurt you." I placed my hand on her leg and noticed it was covered in blood.

I immediately looked at myself in the mirror on my dresser. For the first time, I saw how serious things were. I looked like I was bathed in blood.

"You look like you went to war, Kelsi. What happened ... pleeease tell me," she cried.

She was right. I did. Still, there was no need to push it in her face. I needed to wash the last thing existing of that nigga off my body.

"Baby, let me go jump in the shower and I'll be right back."

"Kelsi, can you talk to me? You're acting strange."

"Let me jump in the shower and I'll talk to you," I said in a calming voice. "I promise, I'll tell you everything later."

"OK Kelsi," she said as she lay down on my bed in the fetal position, pulling the sheets over her body.

I grabbed a few things from my drawers and closed the door. Delonte was on the phone and I knew he was telling my Moms what he thought he knew.

"Couldn't wait to get on the horn, could you nigga?" I didn't really expect an answer.

He just shrugged his shoulders. I didn't care because she was gonna find out sooner or later. I just had to think of what to tell her.

In My Bed
11:15 pm

I cut the lights out with the exception of the lamp on my dresser. I turned on 96.3 FM, a slow jams radio station to relax my shawty. I knew a lot had happened over the past few days and I was barely grasping everything, so I could imagine how it felt for a girl. And then that old school joint by Prince called *The Beautiful Ones* came on. The mood was getting just right.

I had my arms wrapped around her, using my body to hold and convince her that everything was OK. I wanted her to feel that I was OK, too, and that I wasn't going crazy. I was still the same Kelsi who walked her to the bus stop after school. I was still the same Kelsi who sexed her like she liked to be sexed, but now, I was the Kelsi who killed her ex-boyfriend, to protect her and to protect us.

"Baby, would you ever hurt me?"

"Girl, you know better than that. I might get mad at you and shit but I would never put my hands on my girl." I kissed her neck, savoring the scent of her skin, finding comfort in it.

"Well you said before that you'd hurt me. You said it twice the other day," she reminded me as she turned around to face me.

"I said that shit because you wouldn't leave when that nigga was trying to put you in his car. I ain't want him touching you and shit."

"You act like he ain't neva been with me before."

I could tell she said that shit to piss me off and it was workin'. I ain't want to hear nothing about her being with him now, or any other time. All I could think about was what that nigga said outside. I wanted to tell her what he said to me, but I wasn't sure if I was really ready to hear the answer.

"Are you sure Charles ain't fuck wit you that day?"

She was quiet.

"Keisha, I asked you a fuckin' question."

Silence.

"Keisha, did he put his fuckin' hands on you?!" I yelled sitting up straight in the bed.

"No Kelsi! Damn, he ain't fuck wit me at all!" Although she was yelling at me, my tensed muscles began to relax.

Good, she ain't tainted, I thought as I looked at her closely. "You ain't lying to me are you?" I asked as I lay in the bed next to her. "Cuz I can't stand a fucking liar."

"No baby."

"So why would you remind me you'd been with him before? Like I ain't know that shit already."

"I'm just playing, Kelsi. Dang! Why you getting all serious?"

"Yeah, well tonight I don't feel like playing."

"Are you scared of him, Kelsi?"

If she only knew. I never feared him, I feared what he could do to me. A man is nothing more than blood and tissue and tonight I proved it.

I could have gotten all pumped since I killed that nigga and said, "Fuck no I ain't scared of that nigga! Especially a dead nigga!" But I didn't. There was no need for all of that, and I didn't want her knowing what was up. I gave her just enough to know that her man was no punk, and if need be, I *could* protect her like I could protect my Moms.

"Naw baby. Trust me, I don't fear *no* man except God."

She must've liked what I said because she turned around, moved into me and pushed her ass against my dick.

I was just getting ready to go for it when that faggot knocked on my door.

"Uh Kelsi, I don't know what you doing in there, but your mother wants to talk to you on the phone."

"What?!"

"I said your mother's on the phone. Open this door."

This nigga had female tendencies and I expected him to call my mother, so I couldn't be mad. I just laughed to myself because I could just see him telling on me. Instead of rushing to the phone like some scared little boy, I decided to fuck his head up a little.

"Naw man. Tell her I'll talk to her later. I'm busy right now."

I knew telling him that would make him madder than it would my mother. Besides, there was nothing she could do now, the damage was already done.

"You should really talk to your mother, man, she's worried."

"She's worried because you made her. Now get the fuck away from my door."

"Kelsi, come out here and get this phone."

"Man, I'm busy! I'll talk to my Moms when she gets here."

I heard his feet sliding back to the couch. I added a little extra so he could run tell that. I directed my attention to the fine-ass girl I had in my bed. I looked at the clock and saw I had a little under two hours before my mother would be home and I wanted to make love. No, scratch that. I wanted to fuck.

"Your mother is going to be mad, Kelsi," Keisha said.

"No she ain't. My Moms know you over here." I told her this although I wasn't sure if she'd be OK with why I carried his ass, especially in front of Keisha.

"She know I'm over here, but she still gonna be mad you ain't come to the phone when she asked you to."

"I'm a grown man," I said, giving extra for my girl. "It's gonna be all right. Worry about this." I pulled her hand toward my dick.

She looked down as her hand circled my dick and she started stroking me to full attention. "You so nasty, Kelsi."

"Girl, you know you like it. Let me show you how nasty I can be."

I turned her over and kissed her lips. She looked at me with her pretty brown eyes and smiled. She knew what time it was. She started taking the boxers off but I told her not to. I wanted to fuck her with them on. They were big enough for me to slide my dick right in and still bang her back out.

Right before I entered her body she said, "Kelsi, how come you don't like Delonte?"

I was blown away by what she asked, but I didn't want to make her mad and renege on the pussy.

"I don't like him cuz he's a bitch and that's my business,

71

Lakeisha. Why?"

"I don't know. He seems cool, that's all."

I grabbed her face hard enough to get her attention, but not hard enough to hurt her.

"Lakeisha, don't be makin' friends with Delonte. He might not be around too long."

She ain't say nothing else, and I left her to her own thoughts. She could have taken it any way she wanted to.

When I slid in and out of my girl's wet pussy, I realized Delonte knocked on the door not only to irritate me, but to playa hate. The only question I had was *why*?

Riding in the cab felt like being in a casket. I couldn't move or reach Kelsi fast enough. It didn't help that the cab smelled liked somebody farted and rolled up the windows. My head was throbbing because I had just given my resignation and whether or not Delonte and I made it, Kelsi was out of control and needed me at home.

Although Kelsi and I were close, I never revealed my past to him. I had done a lot of shit I was embarrassed and ashamed of, but tonight, I would reveal everything to him. He needed to know that his 31-year-old mother was not a stranger to the pressures of the world.

I knew that sometimes people had a tendency to fuck with folks and force them to say and do things that they normally wouldn't do, but you never take shit out on your own family. But tonight all shit's gonna hit the fan. I chose to hide my past because I wanted to get him away from that life, my life. Hell, I didn't want him even curious about it. Now that I thought about it, maybe knowing about my past could save his future. That's why I took precautions, little precautions, to make sure he'd be OK.

"That will be $15.60. Cash please," the driver said.

It seemed like when I was thinking about reaching *just* Kelsi, it took the driver forever, but now that I was thinking about revealing my past, we were there already. Maybe I was really afraid and was trying to convince myself that I wasn't.

"Ma'am, did you hear me? It's $15.60 please."

The driver was rude and for real, he had a muthafuckin' attitude. His cab and his breath smelled awful. I took my time looking through my purse to pull out exact change. When I found it, I handed it to him. No tip.

"Thank you, Ma'am!"

"You're fucking welcome!"

I slammed the car door dramatically and ran up to my apartment building.

Normally I would have gotten my mail, but there was no delivery greater than the one I had to give to Kelsi. When I walked through the door, Delonte wasn't there. I didn't really care because maybe it was best that Kelsi and I had the place to ourselves, but then I remembered that it was the weekend, and Lakeisha was probably still over. Shelly told me all the time that it was crazy for me to allow two minors to have sex in my house. Like we weren't two minors having sex in *my* house with Lorenzo. That bitch was 50/50. I looked at it like boys will be boys and I'd rather he be *safe*, in every sense of the word, than unsafe in somebody else's house.

I threw my purse and keys on the kitchen table. Suddenly I felt constrained by my own message and hated that it would be delayed due to his girlfriend being there. I opened his door and a strong odor of sex filled the air. I flicked the light on and there they were, lying under the covers.

"Ma, what are you doing? This is my room."

I just stared at him. I was tired of his disrespect and bullshit. I worked two jobs to keep a roof over our heads and I felt he didn't care. I had no idea that when he said he'd be willing to kill someone for me, that it was me he was talking about. The shit he was doing was driving me crazy and definitely drive both of us to an early grave.

"Lakeisha, get up and go into my room," I said slowly, never taking my eyes off of Kelsi.

"Yes Ms. Stayley." She tried to fix her clothing that I'm sure my son messed up. As she walked past me, I noticed a wet stain on the front of the shorts she was wearing. Looking from the stain to Kelsi, he could tell I was pissed because his eyes quickly diverted from mine. I talked to that boy many times about using protection and from the looks of it, either the condom broke, or there was no protection involved.

Once Keisha was out of the room, I looked down at my hand. I didn't realize that I was carrying the bat I kept by the door. Some instincts come back, even when you don't know it. Although I felt like fucking Kelsi up for his disrespect, I knew he was still a man who was capable of whooping my ass.

"Ma please calm down," he said in a low voice as he stood on his bed.

"Sit the fuck down! We have to talk and we have to talk now!"

"OK Ma, but can you calm down please."

"Kelsi … you're not giving any more orders around this fucking house. Now sit the fuck down!"

When he wobbled his way into the sitting position on his bed, I grabbed the chair and sat in it backward, with one hand on the back of the chair and the other on the bat. I looked him dead in his eyes. I wanted to evoke all of the things I hid from myself in him. I wanted him to know that although he had height on me, that was about it. I saw more shit in my day than he'd see in his entire life. Without saying a word, I knew Kelsi had a glimpse of my violent past, and it scared the hell out of him.

"When Delonte told you I wanted to talk to you, why didn't you get your narrow ass on the phone?" I questioned slowly as I tapped the bat on the floor.

"Ma … uh … I didn't get on the phone because … uh … Delonte was bothering me," Kelsi stuttered.

"So let me get this straight. You didn't get on the phone, although it was me, because Delonte was bothering you?" I kept my voice low. I knew raising my voice would remind him of the old me, and I wanted to break the tradition, at least for tonight. I didn't want him to know what to expect.

"Ma, it wasn't like that. Can you please put the bat down?"

"Kelsi, if I put this bat down, it'll be on the top of your head."

His look was that of confusion and mine was that of rage. I was giving him a taste of the hood that was still in me, because it never left my soul.

"Kelsi, I'm your mother and you had no right disrespecting me tonight. I was scared, and afraid something had happened to you. Delonte —"

"That's what I'm saying Ma, he worried you, not me."

"Interrupt me again," I said as I took three breaths so deep, my nostrils flared. "And I'll knock the fuck out of you with this bat." Kelsi's eyes got wide because he knew when I used a cuss word, I wasn't playing; well, whenever I cussed at him anyway. "See I know you're a man now. I can see you, Kelsi, I have eyes. I don't claim to be able to whoop your ass anymore with my bare hands, but I can knock you the hell out with this bat. Do I make myself clear?"

"Yes Ma'am."

Yes Ma'am. I liked that. I had only been here for five minutes and I was already making progress. I continued where I left off.

"Whatever beef you have with Delonte, eat it!" I said, looking at him. "Because it doesn't excuse you for disrespecting me. You will respect me even if you don't respect him. Kelsi, let me tell you a few things about your mother that you *don't* know. I think when I talk to you sometimes, you think I'm talking out the side of my neck. The shit I'm trying to instill in you has been lessons I've learned personally. I never told you this before, but before my daddy died, he made me have sex with every one of my brothers. He told them that the best way to learn how a woman worked was to be with one. I was only 11 years old and I had all of them, including my father. One by one they climbed on top of me whenever they got the urge. For years I felt used. All I wanted was for my daddy to protect me, and instead, he turned his back."

Kelsi squinted his eyes as they filled with tears. Determined not to let me see them drop, he turned his head. I knew it hurt to hear his grandfather and his uncles had raped me, especially since he never knew them. I turned his head toward me and continued speaking.

"He loved the boys, Kelsi. He loved all four of my brothers. I'd hear him all the time saying, *Watch your back. Never let them see you sweat. Walk with your head up.* I've told you many of the things I've heard him say to them, and a few other things I've learned in the past. Although he wasn't talking to me, and could care less about me, I listened anyway. When I was strong enough to leave, at 13 years old, his words were all I took with me. My Moms tried to help me but she was too weak. One day, she handed me a Crown Royal bag filled with change. As I took the bag from her, her fingers touched mine and we both stared at each other. Her eyes were filled with so much pain. When she couldn't stare any longer, she blinked, and I saw a tear roll down her left cheek. She pulled me close to her, told me she was sorry, kissed me and told me to go as far away as I could. Kelsi, she kissed me ... me! For weeks I didn't wash my face because it was the first time she'd ever shown me any type of affection. The day she left him was the day I contacted her but I never saw him or my brothers again.

"I ran with a group for years called the Monopoly Honeys. We stuck people up, jumped girls and even stabbed a few folks. I was involved in a life so dark, telling you *everything* could possibly endanger your life. I learned quickly and the streets protected and looked after me. I could sense when danger was near but I was so involved in that lifestyle, that I went into it anyway.

"Men came in and out of my life, taking from me what they could. My dignity and self-respect were the first things to go. All I wanted was a man to be there for me and I didn't care about nothing else but it never happened. Not even when I met your father. He made me do everything from stabbing women who owed him money to selling my body to settle deals he had with people he owed and Shelly was right there, too."

I realized I was giving him a lot, but I couldn't stop. I felt if I stopped to think about what I was saying, I wouldn't say anything. It killed me to see the tears form in his eyes and run down his face but what I was telling him needed to be told.

"I always thought he loved Shelly more than me. Your father that is. He met me first and I still felt she was his favorite. I found out later that he beat her every single day they were together. He beat her because she wasn't willing to do everything I did to prove her love. It's because of his bullshit that Lorenzo Jr.'s slow. He beat her so bad that she had complications with her pregnancy."

Kelsi reflected on his limited interactions with Lorenzo Jr. He knew something was wrong, but never could have imagined that his father caused that boy's problems.

"He didn't have that problem with me. I was the *Down Ass Chick* you hear on the radio all the time. Some of the worst things I did happened in New York. I dealt with a man who sold me out to protect himself, and he almost killed me, Kelsi! This muthafucka shot me and threw me in the back of his trunk just to protect his ass. If it wasn't for me running into the right person, I'd probably be dead right now, so I've been in the streets and know what I'm talking about," I said as the flashbacks of my past haunted me for a few seconds.

"I could have easily gone back to a lifestyle of slinging and dealing, but I work my ass off so you can be safe, Kelsi. I work my ass off so you don't have to be in somebody's trunk or on somebody's corner like I was. The thing about that lifestyle is you are never truly free of it. Trust me son, the hood is alive and lives in me. If you ever disrespect me again, you'll get a chance to see it. I swear until I take my last breath on this earth, you will."

Kelsi wiped his tears with his hands but his eyes were still red. He looked down at the floor and up at me again.

"I have to tell you something, Ma."

"What is it?" I asked, wondering if he understood what I was saying.

"I killed someone today."

There was silence. I felt heavy. My mind wandered everywhere. I wondered where Delonte was. I wondered what we were going to eat tomorrow. Damn, it's hot in here. Did I lock the door? My mind started racing to everything else but what my son just told me. I felt if I thought about something else, it would erase everything he said, including his confession of murder. Although in my heart, I had a feeling something major happened the moment Delonte described how he acted and looked when he came home tonight. I'd been around it too much in the past.

"Ma. Did you hear me? I murdered this dude named Charles Rick."

I was trying to think about what I was going to say. My thoughts were all over the place and I needed to convey the right message to my child. Whatever that meant. The conversations I was prepared to have with my son were for pregnancies, marriages and even hustling … but not murder.

"Kelsi, what happened?"

"Remember when I came in with the stitches the other day?"

I didn't move because shaking my head would've possibly confused me and I needed to understand everything he was saying.

"Well, he took the end of his gun and beat me with it that day."

"Who is he?"

"The person I killed."

"Go ahead, Kelsi."

"*Well* … I wasn't playin' no ball, but just so you know, niggas play touch football on the concrete all the time, I don't care what Delonte says."

"But why, Kelsi?" I asked, feeling good that I was coming back to reality. "Why did he hit you with the gun?" I asked, not entertaining his touch football comment.

"I don't know why, Ma. He's been fucking –"

His eyes grew big because he realized he cussed in front of me again, but what he was telling me was so serious that cussing was the only way to describe the reasons for taking another person's life.

"It's cool. Go ahead, Kelsi."

"Well, he'd been messing with me since last year. I don't know why and he didn't give me a reason but yesterday things got out of control. We fought and he had a gun and used it to hit me. Well tonight, I came home and he was in front of our house, Ma. He went too far. I ain't want him hurting you or me so I did what I had to do."

"Hurting me? Why would you think he'd hurt me?"

"Because he was the one who spoke to you that night you came home."

A flood of fear took over me for a second. I was totally unaware that anything was going on and that would have been a perfect opportunity for him to come after me.

"So the boy with the scar," I paused. "The one who was outside the other night, is the one you killed?"

"Yes. And I would've killed him then if he hurt you."

It felt good to know that he was thinking about me, but it could have just been the euphoric feeling I felt because the blood was rushing to my head instantly due to everything that was happening. I also realized Kelsi was lying his ass off. Every man on earth who has ever had a beef knows why, and he was no exception. Kelsi was doing an awful job of lying to me and for that one moment, his real age came through. But asking him why and probing him for questions wasn't going to help the situation, so I left it alone.

"Kelsi, where's the body?"

Damn, where did that come from? I know I said the hood was still in me, but now it had taken over. Suddenly I was concerned with separating any connection between my son and the dead body. I was worried about forensics.

"Uh, I put him in the dumpster. I took his clothes off and put them in the bag under the bed. I kept the gun, too."

I smiled inside because he was using his head. He was more careful than I thought.

"Good, Kelsi. Does anyone else know but me?"

"I didn't tell no one, and I mean no one."

I knew he was referring to his girl and that comforted me. A little.

"Are you sure?"

"Positive, Ma." he assured.

"Because that would cause major problems."

"I know."

"OK, we're going to burn the clothes in the bag. Do you remember him scratching you or anything?"

"No, not really," he said in a low voice.

I knew DNA was a muthafucka and if the body had any on him, anything we did to dispose of the body would be null and void if it were found.

"OK. You're going to go to school as normal. Don't do any-thing different, Kelsi. Go the same places you go and do the same things you do. The cops will come around because I'm sure someone has seen you two fighting, even if you don't know who they are. Someone will talk, maybe even somebody close to you." I was giving silent implications toward his girlfriend. "But stay strong, baby. Don't crack and remember that now that you've committed the ultimate crime, the streets are watching."

I stood up and put the chair back where I got it. I walked toward the door and before turning around to look at him, I softened my face. I felt it was time to bring back his mother, instead of the gangsta bitch I just introduced him to, because he needed her more than ever. I turned around and said, "Kelsi, I love you. Don't worry, together they can't fuck with us. Trust me."

He let out a half smile and I opened the door. When I did, Delonte was standing in the doorway. I wondered how much he'd heard.

A Hustler's Son

When I woke up I had the worst taste in my mouth. It tasted like I'd been smoking and ate the butts at the same time. My head felt like I'd walked on it all night. The alarm clock was ringing and I couldn't pull myself up to cut it off. The sound was becoming so excruciating, that each *bomp bomp bomp bomp bomp* felt like someone was knocking me in my head.

"Delonte. Delonte. Can you cut the alarm off for me?"

"What?" he said with his heavy morning voice.

"I said, can you cut the alarm off for me?"

"Come on, Janet. You're closer. Cut it off yourself."

I couldn't stand him sometimes. Still lying on my stomach, I pulled myself up like a newborn baby trying to raise her head for the first time, and slammed my hand down over the alarm clock. When I was sure it was off, I plopped back down on the bed.

I almost knocked the empty glass over, that at 2 o'clock in the morning, was filled with the Grey Goose Vodka I had been drinking.

I guess I was hoping to drink myself back into a time before any of this happened. I couldn't imagine my baby going to jail, and I couldn't imagine somebody killing him. I didn't know

83

what to expect because Kelsi hadn't told me *everything* that happened, but I was ready.

Whoever tried to take him from me had to take me first. I spent all night talking to Delonte and trying to figure out how much he had heard. I'm sure the drunker I got the more obvious I became. So if he didn't hear anything, my bad acting job definitely let him know we were having an intense conversation in his room. After all, why else would Lakeisha be in our room?

He swore up and down he just got there when I opened the door, but something in his eyes told me different. He had a look of satisfaction on his face. It was almost as if he had one up on me, on us. I couldn't do any of this now. I had to go back to sleep.

Still In Bed
12:15 pm

I rolled over and put my hand on the space where Delonte had been. Where was he? I opened the drawer next to my bed and pulled out the pack of BC Powders. Removing one from the box, I opened the cellophane paper and poured the powdered substance into my mouth. I used remnants from the liquor in my glass to wash it down. They're the only thing that worked for my headache. I sat up straight in the bed and nestled my feet in the carpet on the floor. It was time to face my day. I desperately needed God's help to do it, too.

I walked toward the bedroom door and stopped short when I heard Delonte on the phone. Hiding behind the door, I stopped to listen to his entire conversation.

"I know something else was up," he said.

He was trying his hardest to talk low but his voice was so deep that even his whispers carried.

"I know, man, and I'm tired of his shit. She pacifies him too much."

I put my ear closer to the door to make sure I was hearing this shit right.

"I'll let you know later. Just answer your phone. Don't do anything now and remember that as long as I'm good, let things be good."

I backed up from the door and sat back on the bed. I didn't know how to take what I just heard and I didn't know what he meant. Was I sleeping with the enemy? Had I let the one man in my home who was out to hurt us, instead of help us? If I'm good, let things be good. What the fuck does that mean? For some reason, the same man I wanted in my life, I wanted out of it.

Five minutes later Delonte walked into the bedroom. He looked surprised that I was up and staring at the walls. He didn't know that the walls, although blank for him, were filled for me with all the shit I had going on in my head. I saw plans for attack and outlines for the days to come.

"I didn't even know you was up," he said in a guilty tone.

"You wouldn't," I let out by accident.

"Now what's wrong? What, you need some more money or something?"

I was trying to be careful, really careful, because I was having old feelings and it was scaring me a little. His lying was infuriating me so badly that in my past, I would have jumped up and slit his throat before he even knew what happened. I imagined how quickly he would hit the floor. With his body weight and size, I guessed it would take no more than 20 seconds.

There was a time in my life when I didn't trust anything anybody said, only the things that they did. I learned to find the code in statements normal people referred to as the English language.

For instance, what *just* came out of his mouth was, "What, you need some more money?" What I heard was, "I'm trying to buy your son's life. How much will it cost me?" Suddenly, it was as if I walked into a closet and put on my old uniform. I was willing to do *anything* I had to do to keep my son out of harm's way.

But how much did he know? Who was he talking to on the phone? I had to outline a plan that controlled his life and left ours out of it. Before I made any sudden moves, I decided to invite him out for a quiet night alone using the same technique he just used on me – bullshit.

"Baby, you don't have to give me nothing, although I did quit my job yesterday like you asked. I was hoping we could spend a little time together tonight, that's all."

"Damn girl, straight up!" He was excited.

"Yeah, I was gonna tell you when I got home last night but I had to deal with Kelsi," I said in a low voice. "You were right about him, it's about time I put him in his place. He's too far out of control. Not coming to the phone when I asked him was the last straw."

There. I said it. I pretended to be against my son for a greater purpose. His eyes lit up like a kid on Christmas day.

"I'm sorry you had to go through that shit, too. I know you were tired as hell last night. Of course I'm down with spending some time with my lady," he said as he hugged me and kissed me softly on my lips.

The man I so badly wanted last week now looked foreign to me. His kisses stung my lips and were bitter to the taste.

"Don't worry about the job, baby, as long as I'm here, you're going to be OK." He reached in his pocket and placed everything he had on the table. I picked up the wad of money right in front of him. I had to see it for myself. I had to see with my own eyes what price he put on my son's life. He wanted me to sell him out, and didn't think I was smart enough to know it. I shook my head and laughed when I counted two grand in cash.

Is two grand the price for Kelsi's life? I thought. Not in my book.

"Thanks, honey. I can pay a few bills in advance with this. I really appreciate it," was all I could manage to say.

"Hey, don't worry about it. We're in this together," he said as he brushed his hand alongside my face.

"You've done a lot for me."

"Don't worry about it, baby."

"I wish I can show you how much I appreciate you," I told him as I rested my head on his stomach as he stood in front of me.

"I do have an idea on how you can show me just how much you really appreciate what I do around here." He stepped back just a bit, unzipped his jeans and released his swollen dick. "Yeah baby, show me just how much you appreciate me."

I hadn't even been off my second job for a full 24 hours and already he was making me prove to him how much I needed him.

What Delonte didn't realize was that I'd played this game before, plenty of times. I played it so much that it no longer bothered me. He was technically my second job. But this job was different because it was only temporary. I knew it but he didn't.

I took him into my mouth and gave him the bomb-ass head. I even let him grab the back of my neck and pump himself into my tongue strokes. It was something I never did before. I sucked and licked him on every inch of his rock hard dick. I twirled my tongue over and along the tip. I sucked him like I needed him to live.

I didn't feel bad because it wasn't me having sex to control the enemy, it was Helena Hope, a two-time felon who was *still* wanted for murder. He just didn't know. But then again, how would he?

Kelsi
Chapter 8
September 18
Sunday, 10:50 am

Walking to the bus stop with Keisha felt weird. I wondered if anybody saw me murder Charles and if they'd be lookin' for me. I really did need a car. Days like this made me hate being a youngin'. Sometimes I wondered why Lakeisha's fine ass was walking with me when she could be cruising with somebody else. There were a few people out doing regular shit, talking, laughing and slangin' coke, but nothing that would make me think I was wanted. Truthfully, I couldn't wait till Keisha got on this bus because I needed time alone. I wanted to clear my mind.

"Kelsi, why you ignorin' me?" Keisha asked with her hand over her eyes to block the sun.

"Keisha, I'm not ignorin' you. Just cuz I ain't talking, don't mean I ain't listenin'."

"*Wellllll*, I asked you what was up with Ms. Stayley. Why she bust in on us like that last night?"

Keisha asked too many questions. It wasn't enough for her to just chill, she had to know the ins and outs.

"Baby, she came in cuz it's her house and she wanted to talk to me."

"Well, it's been her house and she ain't never bust in like

that before."

"Well, she did it last night, so stop fuckin' trippin'!"

I swear, Keisha was pissin' me the fuck off. I felt like knockin' her ass out. I had too much shit on my mind and then to have her playin 20 Questions, man, I was about to snap. I just killed a muthafucka, my Moms tripped out on me, and my shawty's mouth was on full.

"Aw no you didn't just talk to me like you lost your damned mind, Kelsi!" Her hands were on her hips and her head was rollin' like only a black woman could do. "Boy, you best act like you got some sense, Kelsi, I ain't scared of you!" Next thing I know, she reached in and smacked the shit out of me.

Keisha has hit me in the past. It was always play taps or when she was mad she might slap me or some shit like that, but today, things were different. I ain't want her touching me. I ain't want nobody touching me. I don't know what came over me, but I took my right hand, grabbed her neck, and pushed her up against the back of the bus stop. She started turning red but I didn't stop. The silence relaxed me, because for right now, the bitch wasn't sayin' shit. I even took a few seconds to think about what I had to deal with back at home. When I finally focused on Keisha, and not on what I was doin', I released the hold I had on her.

When the sound of a motorcycle driving down the street passed us up, I realized what just happened. What the fuck was I thinking? Why was I choking the life out of my girl at the bus stop? Just yesterday I wanted to protect her and now I wanted to kill her. I immediately released her and tried to console her. But how do you go from choking somebody to asking them if they're OK? She probably really thought I was crazy now. The thing is, I didn't know if I was or not.

"I'm sorry, baby. I'm sorry. I tripped out for a second, I'm so sorry," I said as I tried to hug her.

She sat down on the bench and pushed me away from her. She placed her hands on her neck, like she was makin' sure it was still there. It was. It just had marks from my hands all around it. She was starin' at me tryin' to figure out what was going on and who I'd become, but I knew as hard as she looked at me, she would never be able to tell what was up. Hell, I ain't even know.

"Kk … elsi," she said trying to catch her breath. "What are you doing? You changed. You ain't nothing … like you used to be." She was on the bench shaking and crying. "What are you going through? Talk to me?"

I paced back and forth and tried to answer her questions, but it felt like the hardest questions I ever had to answer in my life. Maybe in a way, I blamed her for all of this shit. I don't know. All I know is two days ago I was a 15-year-old kid doin' regular shit, now I was a felon.

"Look, maybe we need some time apart, Keisha. Shit is real fucked up for me right now. I ain't tryin to hurt you, but if you stay wit me, I probably will."

I didn't know where that came from but it was true. Maybe the same person who killed Charles said it, and he was right. The way I was goin', I could snap at any given moment. I felt like two people were living inside of the same body, one was Kelsi Davis and the other was a cold-blooded murderer who was nameless.

"Kelsi," she said in a low voice. "I ain't tryin' to lose you. Maybe I was talking too much, maybe you needed to think and I ain't let you. It's cool. I'm still breathin'."

There she was. My shawty. I almost killed her and she was still trying to be with me but that ain't do nothing but *really* make me want to call it quits. Somebody down for me like that deserved to be safe, and if she stayed with me, I couldn't guarantee it.

"Kelsi, do you love me? Cuz right now, you actin' like you don't."

Silence.

"Kelsi … do you love me?"

I looked at her face and it was soaked in tears and all I could think of as I walked away without answering was, it's better than blood.

Kelsi
Chapter 9
September 19
Monday, 2:30 am

I thought I was dreaming when I felt my Moms come in my room. She'd been in and out telling me that Lakeisha kept calling, but I didn't want to talk to her, at least not yet. When I glanced at the clock on my dresser, I saw it was two thirty in the morning. Keisha knew better than to call me that late. Moms would have cussed her ass out, and me too, so what was going on?

"Kelsi, Kelsi, we got a problem, baby, wake up." I felt a soft but firm touch shaking me.

"What's up, Ma?"

"We may have to kill Delonte." Moms was in the dark with nothing but the light from the LCD clock shining on her face.

I heard her but I didn't. The last time I saw her in my room this time of night, outside of busting in on me and Keisha the other night, she woke me up to give me this coat I'd been stressin' over. To this day I don't know how she knew I wanted the coat because I didn't tell her or my father. But she came in my room at three somethin' in the morning like she was doing now. When I woke up, she took me to the living room and showed me this four hundred dollar North Face coat I wanted. She'd worked overtime to get it for me and everything.

I loved my mother more that day for buying me that coat. Not because she spent the money for it, or because we really didn't have it, but because she cared about my feelings. She was like that, always caring about my feelings. But something in me told me tonight wasn't about a coat.

"Ma … what did you say?"

"I said we have to kill Delonte."

"What he do to you? Did he hurt you?" I yelled as I got up and sat on the edge of the bed, while cracking my knuckles.

I was wide awake now. If he touched her, he'd most certainly sealed his fate.

"He didn't do nothing to *me*. It's because of what he wants to do to *you*."

Now I was confused. How she go from being in love with him, to wantin' to take him out, and what did I have to do with it? I thought I was dreaming so I tried to focus on her face to see if what she was telling me was real.

"I don't understand, Ma. You got to give me more than that."

She stood up and started pacing. My eyes moved with her, just in case she made any sudden moves. I mean, I wouldn't hurt my mother, but she *was* trippin'. She picked up one of the framed pictures I had of her on my dresser, cut the lamp on and sat back in the chair.

"Do you know where I took this picture, Kelsi?" she asked as if she never asked me to kill her boyfriend.

"Um, I think you took it at a park or something."

"No, Kelsi. I took this picture at a picnic area, in front of a clinic. An abortion clinic. Shelly took it for me. I was three months pregnant with you and your father was trying to get me to have an abortion. I was only 15 years old and wanted to be with him, so I agreed I would, but when I got there, I just couldn't do it." She stared at the picture and smiled. "I ain't want nobody taking you from me, but even then, somebody was try-

93

ing to split us up."

She handed the picture to me as if I never had seen it before. I'd seen that picture many of times because I looked at it every day. I could tell her every detail in that picture, except where it was taken. I took the picture from her and put it back on the dresser.

I folded my hands with my elbows on my knees and looked into her eyes.

"Ma, I need you to tell me why you're askin' me to do this. This is serious. You ain't just ask me to whoop his ass, you askin' me to kill the nigga. Now I know Delonte don't care for me, and truthfully I don't care for him either, but I ain't tryin' to kill him."

I knew I was wrong for cussing, but she was askin' me to murder, and as far as I was concerned, for now, one cancelled the other.

"Kelsi, Delonte heard our conversation the other day. You know, when Keisha was here. He heard you admit to murdering that boy."

"What, how do you know?" I asked as I stood up. "Did he say it? Did he actually say he heard us?"

"Well, yesterday I heard him on the phone talking to somebody and I could tell the conversation was about you. I decided to see how much he knew, so we went to dinner." She stopped talking as she was trying to follow me with her eyes while I paced the floor. She continued, "He took me to Moe's in Baltimore and we talked about a lot. Anyway."

Yeah, get to the point, I thought, although I didn't say it.

"I started questioning him about a few things. You know, tryin' to hint around to see how much he heard. What he said toward the end confirmed he knew everything."

"What he say, Ma?"

She was makin' me mad. I hated when she dragged the story

out. Get to the point!

"His exact words to me were, *'I heard what I heard but I ain't sayin' nothing. Tell Kelsi everything will be OK. His secret is safe with me.'* It sounded good, but knowing how he feels about you baby, I know he gonna say something, and I can't have that. I don't want you doing time in no fucking prison! It just ain't happening."

"So what did you say? I mean, does he think you know he knows?"

"Naw, I tried to make him think that Keisha was pregnant or some dumb shit like that, but I know he's not buying it."

"What did he say, Ma? How do you know he wasn't going for that?" I asked, wondering why that lie wouldn't work.

"Because he said to tell you congratulations on the baby, and that he's happy to hear that it's that because he could've sworn he saw death in your eyes the night you came in. He also said he thought you wanted him to see it."

I sat back down on the bed, and stared at her. I was listenin' but to me, seeing death in my eyes didn't mean he deserved to be killed. Based on what Ma said, I wasn't sure if he knew shit. Maybe he wanted her to think he knew something, just to fuck with her and see if she'd talk. "Ma, I think killin' him is going too far," I whispered, especially since I didn't know where he was in the house.

The concerned look she had for me turned into rage.

"Kelsi Davis," she said real slow, through clenched teeth and her finger pointed in my face. "I am telling you now, I want him silenced!! There's no need to question what I'm askin' you to do, just do it!"

"Ma, you're askin' me to kill somebody. I got to question you about that."

"You didn't have no problem killin' that boy did you? Killing Delonte is needed to cover your tracks. Sometimes you'll have more than one casualty in war."

More than one casualty in war? What the fuck was Moms talking about? Just because I killed one person ain't mean I wanted to go on a killing spree. I could tell she was upset, and I hated it, but I couldn't kill nobody else, especially with me *just* killin' dude. I wanted all this shit to go away. I'm not a serial killer. I understood that she didn't want to lose me, but if I followed her plan I'd most certainly be getting locked the fuck up.

"Ma, I can't do that. Let's let things blow over first and talk about this later."

She got up, put the chair back where she got it from and turned around to look at me.

"You can't leave a job half done, Kelsi. Remember that." She walked out of my room and closed the door behind her.

Kelsi
Chapter 10
September 19
Monday, 1:45 pm

I was rolling a pencil back and forth on my desk. *You can't leave a job half done, Kelsi. Remember that.* My life had really changed. I started rolling my pencil again. I pushed it to the left, and it moved. I pushed it to the right, and it moved again. For a second, I needed to have control over something in my life because right now, all other aspects of my life were out of control.

"Mr. Kelsi William Davis, if you'd like to continue to interrupt the class by not participating, I suggest you leave. Contrary to what you may believe, *some* people would like to complete their assignment."

I was getting ready to cuss that bitch out when I noticed through the window in the door that people were going back and forth in the hallway causing a lot of commotion. That nosey bitch Ms. Temples was complaining about me, and they were just parlaying in the hallway. She decided to see what was up. Before she made it to the door, Mrs. Swagles, the office administrator, made an announcement over the intercom.

"Excuse me Bladensburg High School students and faculty, we have a terrible announcement to make." Her voice was sad and shaken. "Charles Rick, a senior here, has passed away.

97

Counselors will be available today and tomorrow for anyone who'd like to talk. Thank you."

They found his body already? Shit!!

The entire class was moving around and going crazy. Ms. Temples sat back in her seat, and dramatically placed her hands over her mouth, acting like she was in complete shock. She looked at us as if she were saying, *You see how upset I am? Make sure you tell your parents.*

Unlike Ms. Temples' fake ass, I slumped all the way down in my seat, trying to avoid any *extra* attention and trying to go unnoticed. I felt if anyone looked at me, they'd know I had something to do with it. His blood was still fresh on my hands and the memory was embedded in my mind.

I took my cap off, wiped the sweat off my forehead and tried to relax. The room was spinning and I was getting hotter and hotter. Calm down, Kelsi. Stop trippin' and calm down! Nothing I said to myself was working. *Don't crack and remember that now that you've committed the ultimate crime, the streets are watching.* This resounded in my head over and over. They hadn't even come for me yet, and already I was breaking down. I decided I couldn't take it anymore and it was time for me to leave. I had to get the fuck out of there.

I cleared my throat and said, "Ms. Temples, may I be excused?"

"No. With everything going on now, I don't think it's safe."

"But I have to leave anyway," I insisted.

"For what?"

"I have to go to the restroom." I lied. I didn't know where the fuck I was going, but for now, I wanted to get out of the class.

"Like I said, it's not safe so take a seat Mr. Davis."

Maybe if I didn't know who killed him, I would have sat back down, or maybe not, since I couldn't stand the bitch. I was the only one in the world who could assure her that whoever killed Charles wouldn't be coming back for me.

"Ms. Temples, I'm tryin' to be respectful by asking, so may I *please* be excused?"

"Mr. Davis, I said no. Now sit down and finish your work!"

"Fuck you, bitch!"

It came out and it couldn't be stopped. I'd thought about calling her out of her name before, and it never slipped, but today it did. Ms. Temples had a thing about embarrassing people that fucked me up. I didn't care for her at all.

"What did you just say?"

Silence.

There was no need to repeat myself because she heard me loud and clear. Everyone stopped talking about Charles and started looking at me. I got my shit together, and was ready to leave.

"I said," she said as if she were singing, "what did you say to me, Mr. Davis?"

She heard what the fuck I said the first time. People killed me when they did that shit. Then when you repeat it, they wanna act all shocked and shit, like they didn't expect you to repeat yourself. If that was her way of tryin' to get me to take back what I said, I ain't have no intentions of doin' it.

"I said, fuck you, bitch," I repeated as I grabbed my dick. "I'm outta here."

I couldn't take it anymore. All she had to do was give me a couple of minutes to clear my mind and to sort things out but she was insistent on embarrassing me and making me look like a fuckin' idiot in class.

I opened the classroom door and bailed out. At that very moment, I felt free. I decided to go home and get my shit together because if anybody asked me what I knew today, I would have definitely lost it.

On my way down the hall, I saw Lakeisha again. I saw her

earlier in first period and she didn't say shit. She had a dress on and everything and her legs were closed shut. I figured she was still mad because I didn't answer the phone last night when she called.

She was going into the bathroom when she saw me. She stopped and looked at me. I acted like I didn't know her and walked out of the double doors.

"So you not talkin' to me no more?"

I turned around and saw her behind me. School wasn't out just because I walked out of class, so I wondered what she was doing.

"Keisha, you betta go back in there. You know they'll suspend you for coming outside during school hours." I started walking.

"Well where you going?" She was walking toward me.

"I'm leavin' for the rest of the day!"

I didn't face her and I kept walking. If I looked at her she would have messed my head up and I needed to focus.

"Kelsi, please talk to me! I need someone to talk to!"

I turned around and pulled my cap all the way over my head so the only thing I could see were her feet. I couldn't face her, I couldn't face anybody. I felt like a sign was on my head that said, "I murdered Charles Rick. Tell everybody!"

"Did you hear? Did you hear what happened to Charles?"

"Umm, uh, yeah … I heard. That's fucked up."

"I know," she said as she sniffled. I couldn't see her face but I could tell she was crying. I couldn't console her because I didn't feel sorry that he was dead, considering I was the one who was looking at the barrel of his gun eye to eye. All I wanted to do was protect my girl, my Moms and myself. I ended the beef the day we punished his ass in the parking lot, but he showed up at my place. Maybe he didn't get the message. If I had to put him six feet deep in order for him to know I wasn't fuckin' around, so be it. He was warned.

"Kelsi, can I ask you something, and promise not to get mad?"

There she go with the questions again. I knew she was goin' to ask me if I had anything to do with Charles being dead, but based on my Moms, the more she knew, the more dangerous it was for her. I decided to do her a favor by ignoring her.

"Keisha, I have to go. I ain't got time for this right now. For real. I'll get at you later." I turned around and started walking again.

"Please, Kelsi!! Give me five seconds, please!!"

I stopped in my tracks and put my hands in my pockets. For her sake, I was gonna try my best to lie to her, but I ain't know if it would work.

"Go ahead, Lakeisha. Make it quick, I got somewhere to be."

"I will." She walked over to me and grabbed my left hand with her right and wiped her tears with the left. "Kelsi, is there somebody else?"

"What?"

"I said, is there somebody else?"

Damn. This girl was tougher than I thought. She never ceased to amaze me. Here it was, Charles was dead, and I'm pretty sure she knew I did it. All she wanted to know is if I was seeing somebody else or not.

"Is that why you crying?"

"Yes," she said as she wiped her tears again. "I miss you, Kelsi."

"You *still* my shawty," I told her, although I wasn't in a mushy mood. "So how can I be fuckin' with somebody else already?"

"Well what's goin' on with you, Kelsi? Why aren't you opening up to me?"

"Keisha … everything isn't meant for you to know. Some

things I don't tell you because I'm trying to protect you."

"But I can handle more than you think I can."

"And I know that," I said as I ran one finger down her face. "That's why I got you by my side. But you also fuck with a nigga when a nigga don't feel like bein' fucked with."

"What's that supposed to mean, Kelsi?"

"Like yesterday, I asked you to let up off a nigga and you kept comin'. You worse than the FEDS, Keisha."

"No I'm not. You wouldn't tell me nothing. Every time I asked you what's wrong, or what's going on, you shut me out." Her voice quivered like she was going to start crying again.

"That's because I don't have to tell you nothing, Keisha."

I knew that hurt but it was the truth. I didn't have to tell her shit. And if she wanted to be with me, she was going to have to accept that.

"Can I leave with you now?" she asked as she hugged me.

"Your Moms gonna fuck you up if she finds out you played hooky today."

"We have less than an hour left before school lets out. They won't even know I'm gone, especially with all the stuff going on in there."

Truthfully, I had a lot of shit goin' on, but I could use her company. No matter how badly I treated her, she was still there. If she wanted to be around me, even after I warned her the other day that I was dangerous, then it was on her.

"You got all your shit with you?"

"All the shit I need." She smiled as she jumped up and down.

"Well, I guess you coming with me."

At the Store
2:16 pm
"Where you callin' me from?"

"I'm on a phone at the corner store by my house."

"Good. When you gonna get a cell, man?"

"I don't know. Everywhere I go is right around the corner, so I ain't thought about it before."

"Yeah well, you need one if you wanna keep workin' for me. Make it happen as of yesterday."

"OK, Skully." I wasn't feelin' his tone but he was always the same. That's one thing I liked about him.

"Well what's up?" he asked.

"Shit is thick around here now. They found somebody dead and the block may be hot for a couple of days."

"Yeah I know, just lay low. You know anything about it?"

I wondered why he asked me that. Although I'm sure I could have told Skully I killed him and why I did it, I decided to keep my business to myself.

"Naw, why you ask me that?" I smiled at Lakeisha coming out the store with a bag of Doritos. Damn that girl's fine!

"I'm askin' because if they start knockin' on doors, I don't need them knockin' on the ones with my shit in 'em!"

"Sorry, man. I don't know nothin' about that."

"Good. Don't ask too many questions, Kelsi. I hear the man in your voice now. I don't know where it came from, but I appreciate it. Just don't let it get in the way of our bizness. And don't ever let it cloud your judgement and make you forget who's really runnin' shit. I put you on cuz I saw the fire in your eyes and you were about bizness, but stay the fuck out of mine."

I heard him, but after what I just did, I felt like I *was* runnin' shit. The more I thought about it, I could be runnin' a lot more.

"OK, Skully. I'll fall back for a couple of days, and keep you up on what's happening."

"Cool. I'm out."

When I hung up the phone I wrapped my arm around Keisha's waist and squeezed her ass.

"You know I'm getting ready to hit that, right?"

"Yeah, I know. Why you think I wanted to come home with you?" She reached down and ran her hands across my dick.

When we reached my building, I saw Kenosha out front. She was sitting in her silver Mercedes CLK320 listening to the radio. The moment she saw me in her rearview mirror, she hopped out with the car still on. I knew she was pressed for me to check her out, because she stayed in the latest gear. I ain't know no female freakier than Kenosha, outside of Keisha's girl Sparkle.

"What she doin' here, Kelsi?" Lakeisha asked. I knew she was about to be real salty the moment we saw her car but I ain't know why her ass was over here. Kenosha popped up whenever she got ready to.

"I don't know what she doin' here, and don't start shit, Keisha."

She knew the old Kelsi, who never laid a hand on her, was gone and the new Kelsi wouldn't have any problems slapping on her ass.

"Whatever, Kelsi," she said as she rolled her eyes.

"I'm not fuckin' playin' with you, girl." I shot back. "Chill out."

Kenosha walked over to us in a black mini dress, with her cleavage showin' and her hair down. Now there weren't too many girls who could stand next to Lakeisha but Kenosha was close. She was 5'7" and had an ass so fat that it was the first thing you saw from the front. She was the truth! With that honey brown skin, thick pretty lips that she kept moist constantly with her tongue, she was definitely a winner.

"Kelsi!" She ran over to me, gave me a hug, and planted a kiss on my cheek. "I miss you, boy!" She kept the kiss there a little longer just to piss Keisha off and it worked.

Lakeisha couldn't stand her and swore she was fake. Her

high pitched voice bothered me a little, but other than that, Kenosha was cool.

"Hey Keeesshu!" Kenosha said as she reached in for a hug.

"Don't even try it Kee-no-show! Let's not even go there. I don't like you and for real, you don't like me. So I'm not about to let you make me fake." She turned around giving me her full attention, and continued. "Kelsi, I'll wait for you in the house. Give me the keys, please." I hurried up and handed her ass the keys before she snatched that girl by the hair.

With girls, if they couldn't stand each other, you'd know it. There were plenty of dudes I didn't fuck wit, but I'd never show it, just as long as they stayed out of my way.

When Keisha was out of sight Kenosha looked at me.

"What in the fuuuuck is wwwroong wit her?!" she said pointing her finger.

"Hold fast, Kenosha. That's my girl," I said, doing the best I could to prevent the disrespect. Why in the fuck she had a problem with Kenosha was beyond me. She continued still drumming up shit.

"What up, Kenosha," I said, not feeding the drama. "What you doin' here?" Now I was free to look her up and down like I knew she wanted me to.

"I'm lookin' for my cuzin boy! Where he be at?"

"I don't know. He should be in the house," I said as my eyes roamed from her titties to her ass.

"No he ain't. I been sittin out here all day waitin'. I hongry and errythang," she slurred as she ran her hands down the sides of her hips.

Damn that girl's sexy.

"And look at you, Kelseeee! Damn you getting big. You ready now," she said looking at me up and down. "You ready for errythang." She walked up to me and grabbed my T-shirt like she wanted to devour me. We were doin' too much in the parking lot but this girl wouldn't stop. All I could do was make sure the blinds in the living room weren't moving with I-Spy, and so far so good.

"Yeah, you getting real big," she said as she ran her hand across my dick.

I usually got mad when women told me I was getting big, because the mind made the man not the body; but for some reason, when Kenosha said it, my dick got hard. Maybe because her hand was on it.

"Yeah, I'm big all right. But you better stop playin' before Keisha fuck you up."

"Boy that little girl bet not fuck wit me," she said as she released me. "It ain't my fault she got somethin' I want." She winked at me and smacked her lips.

Kenosha was sexy but so fuckin' stupid. When you talked to her, all you thought about was fuckin' her because she wasn't good for anything else. You couldn't have a conversation with someone who broke up every word. Don't get me wrong, I use slang like the next nigga. But Kenosha's ass couldn't even hold an Ebonic conversation. She made up words on top of words.

"You not ready for this."

"Don't play with me boyee cuz if you ready for a *reeaal* woman, I'm game."

We were in the middle of a conversation when she heard a song on the radio, and ran to her car to turn it up.

"Ooooooh shit, Kelseee!! That's my shit!! And you don't eeeben fuckin' know what I be doin' when I hear my shit, Kelsee!"

In the middle of the parking lot, she was blastin' Kanye West's *Gold Digger.*

"Now I ain't say she's a gold digger. But she ain't messin' with no broke nigga." She was singing loud as shit. And finally she was forming sentences.

"Kenosha!" I yelled. "Turn that shit down, man!"

She looked so stupid dancing around the parking that she almost got my dick soft. *Almost.*

"Look, I'll tell Delonte you came by," I said trying to get rid of her.

There was no need for me to tease myself with her ass in the parking lot when I had pussy already waiting for me.

"Ooookayyy, Kelsey." Kenosha had a tendency to drag out words and she was doing it again.

"Now let me go see about my girl."

"You need to be seeing about these." She squeezed her titties with my hands, and jumped in the car. I shook my head, smiled and walked away. I ain't fuckin' with that girl. I just like lookin' at her. So I thought.

I realized my dick was still hard fucking with Kenosha when I opened my building's door. Shit! Keisha was gonna flip if she saw me like this. What I saw next immediately made me soft. Two plain-clothes police officers with badges hanging down their necks were walking down the steps. One was a model-type nigga and the other was white. My heart almost dropped, and I wondered if I shoulda taken off running, but they passed me without confrontation. Keisha was standing in front of my door with it slightly open staring at a card in her hand.

I walked up to her. "What they want? What they want, Keisha?" I asked as I grabbed the card out of her hand.

She just walked into the apartment. I knew then that she had said something she shouldn't have, but what I didn't know was what she said. I followed her inside and closed the door.

Janet
Chapter 11
September 20
Tuesday, 5:20 pm

I made the decision when I left work today that I was never going back. There are plenty of other things for a woman like me to do and anything is better than working a 9 to 5. So now having left my first and second job, I was officially unemployed and loving it. I tried to be a better person for Kelsi, and even kept a stable job, but once he got caught up in the game, I had to reprioritize things. I realize quitting jobs and prioritizing sounds crazy but when it comes to working all hours and not being able to see Kelsi as much as I used to, the decision was easy. I had over six grand saved and had a few connections. With those two things going for me along with the plans in my head, I was going to turn the lifestyle that woouldn't let me go into an empire for me and my son.

When I walked into the apartment, I wondered why Lakeisha was there on a school night. I had planned on telling Kelsi I quit my job, and to see if he gave any more thought to taking Delonte out. If he didn't do it, I had all intentions on doing it myself because whether Kelsi understood it or not, it had to be done.

Kelsi's door was open and I saw Lakeisha sitting on the bed crying. Instead of consoling her, Kelsi looked pissed. When the door closed seconds later, I wondered if they were doing it for privacy. They must have gotten into a fight and she came over here to talk to him about it. I never cared much for her, and with everything going on, I cared for her even less. One day, Kelsi looked me dead in my eyes and said, "This one's for me, Ma. Be easy on her." I tried, but she was too needy and required too much attention. With everything was going on, that type of person could be dangerous.

I put my purse down and went into the kitchen to grab the orange juice and the vodka to make myself a drink. Kelsi and Lakeisha were so involved in a conversation, they began to get louder. I grabbed a glass, rinsed it out and made my own Screwdriver. I even added a few cubes of ice and they still didn't hear me. Something had definitely happened. I downed over half of the drink just standing in the kitchen and made myself another. That's when I heard Kelsi say, "But Keisha, why in the fuck would you tell 5-O I was fighting a dude who was killed?! It makes no fuckin' sense!"

The glass I was drinking from slipped out of my hand and shattered all over the kitchen floor. I walked briskly over to Kelsi's door and put my ear up to it. I was concerned with what was happening on the other side of that door. *Damn, what were they talking about?* I wondered as I pressed my ear closer to the door. My heart beat so fast, it nearly felt as if it were coming out of my chest. *Fuck that, I'm going in!*

Kelsi jumped up when I appeared in his doorway. When Lakeisha saw me, she balled up on his bed and covered her face. It was as if she were trying to hide whatever she did from me but I saw right through her. *Bitch! Bitch! Bitch!* What have you done to my son?! I was silent on the outside but on the inside I was lashing out. Something was wrong and she had everything to do with it.

"Ma, uh, the police came by here today. Uh, and Keisha told

them something she shouldn't have."

That much was clear, I thought. I was getting ready to ask him if they questioned him about the murder but I remembered Keisha wasn't *supposed* to know anything. I was hoping that Kelsi kept it that way. I was hoping that he didn't share anything with this idiot that would make her a weapon.

"The police? The police came by for what?" I asked, trying to alert Kelsi to not say too much around her while still trying to find out what she already said.

Kelsi shook his head slightly and hunched his shoulders to acknowledge that he knew what I was doing.

"Oh, the police came by to ask about a dude that went to my school who was killed. They were askin' people around here if they knew or heard anything. I think he was found around here somewhere."

"That's terrible," I said, trying to pretend I didn't know anything either, and trying to show compassion about a person I could care less about. "Well why you be mad at Keisha?"

"You know I came in here the other day all messed up after scrappin' with this cat right, well, turns out it was the same person who was killed."

"What?! They don't think you had anything to do with it, do they?" I was laying it on thick, but it was just to prevent myself from having to kill her. The less she knew, the better.

"Naw Ma, they were just askin' questions."

"So what happened?" I asked in a frustrated manner. In my mind if they didn't know anything, and she didn't say anything, what was the goddamn problem?

"Well she told 'em we got into a fight and that was the last time she saw him. She said the cops said somebody already told them about the fight. I'm mad at her because she shouldn't have said anything."

I looked at Keisha who was still balled up on the bed. I was five seconds from snatching her by her hair and kickin' her fuckin' ass out, but I had another plan for her. See, I knew in this world, nothing controlled more shit than pussy. Whether he knew it or not, hers had control over him, so what better way to make a man despise a woman more than to make him think someone has taken it away? I decided to deal with her in my own way.

"Oh, I see," I said as I nodded to Kelsi. "Keisha, maybe it's time for you to leave, baby. I need to talk to my son alone, and don't worry, everything is OK," I added for free.

"Oh, OK Ms. Stayley," she said in between wiping her tears even though new ones continued to fall.

"I'll talk to you later, Kelsi, and I can walk myself to the bus stop. It's not a problem."

That was funny because Kelsi wasn't going anywhere anyway.

When I was sure she was gone, Kelsi and I had a long talk, and it was a talk he probably didn't want to hear.

Kelsi
Chapter 12
September 21
Wednesday, 7:45 am

Going to school today had me fucked up. Moms had called up to the school and spoke with the principal. She told them I was under a lot of pressure, and that's why I went off on Ms. Temples yesterday. I wish she hadn't done that, because now she'd been looking at me like I was a fuckin' science project.

The moment the door to my building closed behind me, and the air touched my face, I knew I wouldn't be coming back the same. For some reason I knew something would be different, but I didn't know what. I still didn't know what set off the turn of events in my life. How did I go from being a hustler to becoming a murderer? And how did my Moms go from being my mother to an accomplice?

I called Bricks and asked him to meet me halfway to school. I wasn't going to tell him anything, really. I just wanted to feel him out and see if he heard anything about me killing Charles' punk ass. If he heard something, in my mind, there wasn't a need for me to set myself up by going to school. I'd just turn around and me and Moms would have to discuss plan B. If he didn't hear anything, I'd walk into school like nothing was going on, which was easier said than done.

I spotted Bricks right away. He was wearing a black shirt

with a hood, which he pulled over his fitted cap. His hands were in his pocket and he was rocking a pair of black Nike boots. When he saw me he walked over to me. I couldn't read his face and his expression looked blank.

"Hey man. What up? Why you want me to meet you?"

I hadn't expected him to ask me why. Damn! What was I going to tell him? That I missed him and wanted us to spend more time together? Shit! I had to think of something quick, before I made myself look even more guilty.

"Man, I wanted to holla at you about Keisha. She's lunchin' big time."

"Oh word? What she doing now? I mean, I thought ya'll would be good now, since somebody put that nigga to rest."

I paused and he looked at me, trying to figure me out, but there wasn't anything there to see. If nothing else, I rehearsed in the house over and over how I would respond if somebody questioned me about that nigga or mentioned his name. It must have worked because he looked away as if he didn't find what he was searching for. Maybe he thought I did it at first, but then changed his mind because he felt I didn't have the heart.

"What man? What the fuck you staring at me for?" I asked, trying to see if he'd tell me something.

"Uh, nothing man, no reason. It's just a coincidence that he showed up dead around the same time we had beef."

Maybe I was wrong. Maybe he did think I had something to do with it. I was mad when I saw we were already at the school, because I wanted him to go into more detail. I kept forgetting the school wasn't far from where I lived. I slowed my pace. I wanted to see if I was reading him wrong or if he really was trying to fish for something.

"Ain't it though? That shit was perfect timing. I guess I wasn't the only one he pissed off," I said as I walked even slower so he would follow suit.

"Yeah, perfect timing. So what's going on with you and Keisha?" he asked as he slowed his step, too.

"Uh, nothing man. They came around questioning everyone in the hood about that cat. Anyway, I fucked around and sent Keisha ahead of me cuz Kenosha was fuckin' with her head," I said as I leaned up against the school building putting one foot behind me on the wall for support.

"Damn! Where's Kenosha, man? You been supposed to hook me up with that piece."

"Bricks, I didn't hook you up with her on purpose. I'm doin' you a favor, man. You can't afford her ass. Trust me."

"See, that's cuz you too busy payin' with dollars and I'd be payin' with dick."

I gave him dap and laughed a little more than usual at his dick joke, because I was happy there was something to laugh about. But for real, that shit he just said was stupid. How the fuck he gonna pay with dick?

"*Well*, the police came over while I was outside rapping with Kenosha, and Keisha gonna tell them I had beef with Charles, and that we got into a fight."

"Oh snap!! What they say to you?" he asked as he balled his fists and spoke through the hole.

"Nothin' man. They walked right past me, but I know they'll be coming back. It's just a matter of time."

"Well," he said as he looked up at me. "You don't have anything to worry about right, so how can they fuck with you? It ain't like you did nothing."

"Yeah, I guess you right," I said, confirming my lie and his doubt. "I ain't have shit to do with it."

"Hey man, ain't that Delonte's truck?" He pointed to the right.

I turned around to see what he was talking about, and sure 'nuff, Delonte was flagging me to come over. I ain't know what the fuck he was doin' at my school because I couldn't stand him, and as far as I knew, he couldn't stand me either. It was the only thing we agreed upon.

"Yeah, let me see what's up with this nigga. I'll get at you later," I said, giving Bricks dap.

"All right, peace," Bricks said and went into the building.

I walked over to his truck wonderin' what the fuck was up. I ain't like seeing that nigga at the house, let alone at my school. As usual, I took my sweet time walking to his truck. I wasn't on this nigga's clock. I was still tryin' to figure out what the fuck was his problem.

"What you doin' here, man?" I asked as I waved my arms dramatically. It was a little extra, but that's how I was feelin' at the time.

"Get the fuck in the truck, lil' nigga."

"Yo Delonte, what the fuck I tell you about disrespectin me?!" I yelled as I paused for a second. "Get the fuck outta here with that bullshit." I waved him off and walked back toward the school.

When I started walking away he said, "It behooves you to get the fuck in this truck. Trust me," he threatened as he nodded his head while looking over the steering wheel.

Now I was curious. I wanted to know what gave him the balls to come up to my school knowing I couldn't stand his ass. I opened the door, put the only notebook and pencil I carried around on the floor, slid in and slammed the fuck out of his door.

"My bad." I laughed. Then I looked at him and said, "What up nigga? Make it quick."

Instead of telling me whatever he had to right off the bat, he pulled off. My body flew back against the seat but I kept it there. I didn't want him to think his speed bothered me. If he knew I was uneasy, he may have started driving stupid and shit and I may have had to steal this nigga in his jaw. We were on the Baltimore Washington Parkway that was five minutes from my school before he started speaking to me.

"What you want to listen to? I got anything you want in my CD changer."

"I want to listen to why the fuck you picked me up from school," I said as I looked at him and then back at the road. "This shit ain't funny nigga, so what's up?"

"Ha ha, you a funny lil' nigga. Well, let me put something on for me then."

When I heard *Pimpin All Over the World* by Luda, I put my head against the seat and looked at him again.

"Yo Delonte, what up man? I ain't got time for your shit! You pulled me out of school and now we're joy ridin' like we fucks with each other like that. Now I want you to stop bull-shitting. Tell me what you want or just let me go."

Silence.

"Did you hear me nigga?! What the fuck is up?"

Silence.

I lost it, and I hate that I did, too. Now he saw I didn't like how he was carrying shit and most of all, now he knew that I knew he had the upper hand. When a nigga is in control, it's best to remain silent. I realized that but for one second I forgot. It's just like what happened when Charles was on top of me with the gun in my face. It fucked him up when I didn't beg for my life. I was silent. Silence is always best. And that's what Delonte was doing to me. He was playing my game.

"Don't fuck wit me man. I'm tellin you, don't fuck with me," I warned.

Delonte didn't say shit, just pushed his foot on the gas and sped down the parkway. We were all the way in the left lane, act-ing like no other cars were on the road, and he moved straight to the right. Muthafuckas were on horns and brakes hard as shit.

I kept pushin' the imaginary brake that was in front of me and none of that shit worked. My toes damn near came out of my Timbs I was on it so hard.

My life was in his hands and he was playin' Russian Roulette with it. I looked at the exit and saw he was taking Benning Road and I'm tellin' you now, as dirty as Benning Road was, it never looked so good. He stopped at the first place we came to, next to some houses on the street.

I ain't gonna lie, he scared the fuck out of me with that bull-shit. I looked around like somebody was coming to explain to me what the *fuck* was going on. Nothing.

"This is what the fuck is up," is how he started. "I lost The Woods last week."

"What?" I asked, trying to regain my composure after the stunt he just pulled.

"I said I lost the fuckin' Woods last week!"

"So you want a shoulder to cry on or what?"

When I saw he wasn't laughin' and I wasn't smiling I said, "And?"

"Well, Skully said I lost it until the heat goes away because of that kid showing up dead. That was a big part of my income, man. You don't even know. With your Moms stayin' in my pock-ets and me havin' my own bills and shit, I can't have that. I know you understand what I'm sayin', little nigga."

This bamma's lunchin! If he seriously thought I gave a fuck he was sadly mistaken. Why should I give a fuck if he hits hard times? My Moms was gonna be good just as long as I was out there. Believe that!

"I told him I can't just stop business over there. Hell, I was pushin' over there before he even came back from New York. This nigga gets mad and tells me to find somewhere else to push my shit, *period*. He wasn't even tryin' to hear me out!"

"Nigga, what the fuck this got to do with me? I ain't Skully!

Tell this shit to him!"

"It got a *lot* to do with you, you greasy head muthafucka! More than you know. I want you to run my business in Autumn Woods. That spot brings me no less than ninety stacks a week and I want you to handle it for me. Don't worry, I'll make sure your pockets are lined."

"How you sound?" I asked.

"Fuck you talkin' about how I sound? I'm offerin' you a chance to be good in The Woods."

"I'm good now."

"Well you getting' ready to be betta!" He said as spit escaped his mouth and hit my face. I swear I was getting ready to haul off and steal this nigga, until he leaned back and lifted up his shirt revealing the handle of his gun. Niggas loved showing their bitches.

"I was bringing Skully more money than he could count," he continued as if he didn't just threaten me. "And he cut me off like it ain't even matter! Well I want a piece of that back, and you gonna bring it to me."

I ain't believe his ass. If he was getting that much cash, how come he still lived in Autumn Woods with us? I mean, I knew that some ballas lived where they worked, but I *still* didn't see him making ninety grand a week. Plus, Skully would've never closed down an operation that was generating that much revenue.

"Maybe you ain't hear me, man. What the fuck does that have to do with me?" I repeated. "You ain't my daddy, nigga. You ain't putting shit in my pockets, and I'm not offerin' you a shoulder to cry on!"

"Your name is all over shit, nigga. I talked to some folks and I know you killed that lil' nigga last week. I got people, too. A few dudes saw you stompin' him at the gates and him runnin' off with your pussy in his car. That's enough to make a nigga want to kill somebody." He was laughin' like he told himself a good joke. I wonder how funny Charles would think it was.

"I need you to move my shit or I'm dropping a dime."

I was facing him 'till he said that shit. But since I wasn't expecting his clown ass to say anything about offing anybody, or about dropping a dime, I needed time to get my shit together before sayin' anything else.

"I don't know what the fuck you talkin' about, partner!" I told him. As far as I was concerned, it was my word against his.

"Nigga, I heard you in the room with your mother. Stop playin' games, you bitch-ass nigga!" he growled.

"Naw man," I said as I sat back in the seat. "You got me all fucked up. I got a kid on the way. That's what we were talking about," I lied, remembering what my mother said she told him.

"Is that right? Well how come I congratulated Keisha and she ain't know what the fuck I was talking about?" he questioned as he started laughing. "She said she ain't pregnant."

See this is what the fuck I be talking about. She wonders why I go off on her ass. Keisha never fucking listens to me. I told her ass not to fuckin' talk to this clown and this is why. The littlest things she says to his ass gets blown up and now my life was on the line.

"Well maybe Keisha ain't want you in our business, man," I retorted, realizing we could go all day at it for all I cared. Because unless he had proof, he could suck my muthafuckin' DICK!

"I got the shirts, Kelsi. With your blood and Charles' mixed. You shoulda burned 'em, man."

Silence. There was the proof.

"I'm listenin'."

"Yeah, I figured you would." He started laughing. "Anyway, I ain't got no intentions of telling nobody you a murderer. Trust me."

I gave that nigga applause and two fake-ass laughs. His punk ass kept talkin' like he ain't even hear me.

"Cuz to be honest, at first I thought you did it but then I said, NAAAWW, that lil' nigga ain't got no heart. But after speaking to your mother, and thinking about the way she was pressin' me to see how much I heard, I knew you had *everything* to do with it. But when she tried to lie by saying she found out that Keisha was pregnant, but acted all calm, I knew I was right all along. But like I said, I ain't got no intentions of sayin' shit just as long as you run for me in The Woods. I know you pushin' Skully's shit, because you ain't bold enough to do a mutha-fuckin' thing in The Woods without his approval."

"And neither are you, that's why you runnin' to me."

"Nigga, shut the fuck up and listen to how the fuck it's goin' down! From now on when a muthafuckin' head approaches you, instead of goin' for the weed, you ask them what they want."

I heard everything he said, even though I zoomed in on this dude yanking the fuck out of this girl. She must have done some fucked up shit to set him off. When she walked back into the house, and he followed her, I directed my attention back at this punk-ass nigga. Looking at something else was the only control I had over anything else at the time. Once again, shit was out of whack for me and I only saw one way out.

"So let me get this straight, Skully played your punk ass close and told you not to run at The Woods no more, and now you want me to risk my neck by going against 'em?"

"Naw, you ain't goin' against him, you just giving the customers what they want."

"Answer this one question. Why should I cross Skully? He ain't do shit to me."

"You keep putting that nigga on a pedestal if you want to."

"I hear all that shit you sayin', but Skully don't want your shit over there no more! And truthfully, I don't think it got shit to do with what you sayin'. I think some other shit went down and now you're labeled. He knows you're bad business, and that's between ya'll. I ain't fuckin' with him like that. Get somebody else. There's other hand to hand cats out there. Ask one of them."

"I'm askin', no, better yet, I'm telling you!" he commanded as he licked his lips and smoothed his whack-ass goatee with his hand. "If you don't fuck with him, I'm fuckin' with you."

I brushed his ass off with my hand, pulled my cap down and sat back in the seat. That's when he threw a card in my lap that read:

Detective Nick Fearson
Prince George's Police Department
Homicide Division

It was the same card Keisha was given by one of them detectives! Shit.

"You know it's not cool to blackmail niggas, right?" I asked, looking over at him. "There's plenty of niggas swimming with fishes on account of this shit right here."

"What you sayin', lil' nigga?"

Silence.

"Now I don't want to fuck with you, Kelsi, but I *will* if you push me. You *will* push my product and you *will* keep your mouth closed, otherwise, we got serious muthafuckin' problems. Capeesh?"

I nodded my head and agreed, although in the back of my mind, there was only one thing left to do. I'd be doing the streets a favor. He was breaking all kinds of rules and codes. Ain't nothing like a snitch and a blackmailing muthafucka, and this pussy was both. Once again, Mama was right.

**Janet
Chapter 13
September 24
Saturday, 11:30 pm**

It had been three days since I quit my job and I hadn't looked back since. It felt so good to sleep until I was ready to wake up, which usually meant around 9 o'clock in the morning. It would have been better if I didn't have to sleep with the man who wanted to blackmail my son, and not be able to say shit about it. I was trying to honor Kelsi's wishes and not say anything about him pulling up at the school, but the only thing that helped was knowing that Delonte's day was coming.

I stepped out of the shower and looked at my body in the steamy mirror. I rubbed my hands over my short soft hair, my perky breasts and along the sides of my waist. I smiled as I realized I would never have to place my body in that hideous housekeeping uniform ever again. I smiled one more time thinking of how my life would change over the next few months.

I sat on the edge of the bed to make an important phone call. I immediately reached for the house phone, but thought otherwise. I reached down and grabbed my purse and fumbled through it to find my cell. I bought Kelsi one the other day too so we could keep in touch with each other. He laughed when I gave it to him, saying it was exactly what he needed.

"Hey, it's me." I paused. "Yeah, things are still going down as planned tomorrow night." I paused again. "I'll get at you later." I ended the call.

When I turned around I saw Delonte standing behind me. He placed his keys on the dresser, pulled off his shoes and walked into our closet. Inside of the closet he took off one of his shirts. "Who was that, and what's still going on as planned?" he asked as he walked out of the closet and stood in front of me.

"Nothing, baby," I said as I walked around him and stood in front of the dresser mirror that he recently purchased. "It's, uh, nothing and it was nobody important." I grabbed my new Tiffany earrings, necklace and bracelet and put them on. "How was your day?"

I picked up the brush and brushed the back of my short hair, the sides, and then the front. I loved wearing short hairstyles because I could wear it spiked, in a wrap or even straight back. No matter how I was wearing it now, Delonte wasn't paying any attention to it. All I saw was curiosity, followed by rage, in his eyes. He knew something was up with me ever since I left Kelsi's room. The murder changed everyone's lives in this apartment. Nobody who lived here would ever be the same. Ever.

He walked behind me, put his right arm around my waist, and I fell into him. "Ummmm," I moaned. "This feels *soooo* nice." I was lying. Lying for me came second nature. Some call it acting, others call it deceit, but I call it tools for survival.

Suddenly he took his left hand and placed it around my throat. My eyes, which were once closed, were now wide open and glued on his reflection in the mirror. He wasn't buying it. He knew something was up and I wasn't as good as I thought.

He looked at me and laughed. I was scared and didn't know what was happening next.

"Now I'm gonna ask you again, who in the fuck were you talking to?" His hand tightened around my throat.

I felt my breaths shortening and decided to use them sparingly. My arms dropped to my sides and something came over me. The look of fear on my face was eaten by anger. Who was he to put his hands on me? He was a sneak and a snake that had set out to steal the only family I had. Although Kelsi didn't give me any details about his blackmailing, sayin' he didn't want to upset me more, I already knew it had something to do with drugs. I knew more about Kelsi's lifestyle than he thought I did.

Delonte stopped smiling when he noticed the look on my face but instead of letting up, he choked me harder. My breathing was constricted and I began to feel lightheaded. I was determined not to die right now and leave my baby alone. Even still, with his hands around my throat, I knew he wanted to scare me, but not kill me. At least I hoped.

"Girl, you hear me? Who in the fuck were you talking to?"

"I know you betta get your hands from around my throat." My words were full of promise as my eyes locked with his.

His eyes widened but he tried to stand his ground. It didn't matter because I still knew he was scared of the strength behind my words.

"And if I don't?"

"I'm gonna blow your dick off," I said as I aimed the barrel of the gun I'd taken out of the drawer and pointed it at his dick.

He backed away and I turned around to face him with the gun pointed in his direction. I walked over to him and pushed him down with one hand on the bed. I knew I wasn't stronger than he was, but I carried extra weight on account of the steel I had in my hands.

He was so scared that his legs were shaking. He didn't have to be. I mean, I had plans to kill him anyway, but not without finding out everything I needed to know. I had a plan and I was going to use my head. I wasn't going to act on emotions like he just did. I still needed him, in my own little way.

"Can you please put my gun down?" he asked.

"I will, but don't *ever* put your fuckin' hands on me again," I said with the gun still pointed at him.

"I know, baby," he said as he spoke to the barrel of the gun instead of to me. "You know how I am sometimes."

"Whatever the fuck! You was wrong as shit for trying to choke me."

"I'm sorry," he said, meeting my eyes briefly before looking at the gun again. "I just wanted to know who was on the phone. I'm not trying to lose my woman."

"I can't tell you who was on the phone because I have a surprise for you tomorrow. And if I tell you who was on the phone, it will ruin the surprise."

"I'm sorry, baby. Can you please put the gun down."

"I will, Delonte, but if we're going to work, you have to ease up. I've quit both of my jobs for you. I'm here every day. I cook, I clean, I fuck you every which way you like to be fucked, what more do I have to do to show you I'm down for you?"

His face softened and I knew he believed me, so I continued. "You know I love you, Delonte. But please, please, please stop being so muthafuckin' jealous."

I said jealous but I knew he was nervous. He didn't know if Kelsi told me what he was doing. See, when you do so much dirt, you don't know which hole you done shit in. Trust me, I know.

"I'm sorry, baby, but can you please put the gun down *now*?"

"Yes baby, I can," I said slowly as I put it back in the drawer.

With my back turned toward him, I continued to brush my hair. He stood up, came behind me and pulled off my towel. He pushed me farther toward the mirror as his hands explored my body. Looking at me through the mirror, he smiled at me as if he were seeing me for the first time. I wasn't surprised at feeling how hard his dick was up against my ass. He turned me around and placed his lips over mine. With my breasts pressed against his muscular chest, he was seriously stroking my ass.

Although I had all intentions of doing what needed to be done tomorrow, I figured there was nothing wrong with enjoying sex with him for one last time. I thought of it as a dead man's *final* wish. Delonte wanted me and I felt it. It wasn't his dick or the sexual connection that let me know how much he wanted me. It was his soul. I was a woman he'd never be able to control. Something in me told me that he was never really mine, but for some reason, I couldn't put my finger on why. Don't get me wrong, I know he cheated, and cheating could have something to do with it. But I had a feeling that, as he looked at me, and as he touched me, he was touching a woman that didn't belong to him. Ever. With that being said, I didn't belong to him emotionally any longer, whether he wanted me or not.

Having sex when your heart wasn't in it was something I'd done before. In fact, in New York I slept with a few of Jarvis' *so called* business associates when I didn't want to. Although it was always business related, I came every time. I turned down the ones I was not attracted to, though. The whole point was to make them happy. If I couldn't stand to look at them, how could I make them happy? Jarvis said he understood and would say, "Whatever works, honey."

It's almost like taking a job that you enjoy doing. I hated being a housekeeper and a waitress and because of it, I sucked at it. Beds weren't made right, and people got their food cold or late. But when I did things for Jarvis, I did them right. So anything he asked me to do I loved. My only request was if I entertained some of his business associates, they had to be visually correct. Meaning they were required to take care of their physical appearance, they must be clean, and I had to be attracted to them. If they weren't, I wasn't doing it, and Jarvis understood that.

I loved the power I had over them more than anything. I knew that even though they were using me for my body, they still needed me. So in a way, I still had the power, and power always made me cum.

Delonte picked me up and I wrapped my legs securely around his body while we were still engulfed in a heated kiss. With his left hand still holding me under my ass, he took his right and unzipped his pants. When I felt him enter my wet pussy, I wound my hips like the second hand on a clock, real slow, but I grinded hard to hit my spot.

With both of his hands under my ass, he held me and pumped in and out of me with swift, hard strokes. I knew he was taking out his frustrations on me for pulling his gun on him and I also knew my blatant disrespect turned him on. He liked the near-death experience just as much as I liked giving it to him. I wondered how much he'd like what I had in store for him tomorrow.

When I felt his body shake, I knew he was getting ready to explode inside of me. Right before he came, he pulled his dick out with his right hand and reached into the drawer with the left. *What is he doing now?* I thought. This was different.

With the gun in his hands, he threw me on the bed, spread my legs open and demanded that I play with my pussy. I could tell he wanted to regain the control I had stolen from him. So as he commanded, I put two fingers inside my pussy and stroked myself. In, out, around and around at a tempo he was studying intensely. I bucked my hips and moaned like I was enjoying it more than he was. Truth was, I was scared. I did what I was told but kept my eyes firmly on the weapon. But my body responded to everything he asked of me.

When he couldn't take it anymore, he climbed on top of me, and put the gun to my head. With my legs opened wide, he violently thrust in and out of me. I was scared, but didn't want him to smell my fear; after all, life as he knew it would be over by tomorrow. This only made me want to do it even more. I just hoped mine wouldn't be over today.

I decided to step it up a notch, and moved my hips as if I needed him and wanted him inside of me. Suddenly my own moans were starting to arouse me and I grabbed his ass meeting his every thrust with conviction. Around and around, up and down, I moved my hips while the gun was still at my head.

"You bitch! You fucking bitch. I should kill your ass right now but your pussy is so fucking good." He was pounding into my body over and over again.

"I know baby, I know this pussy is good and it's all for you, baby," I moaned.

When I felt myself tingling I knew what was getting ready to happen. *How could this be happening?* I thought to myself. Under this crazy-ass circumstance, I was on the verge of cumming. I decided with that gun to my head or not, if I was gonna die, this would be the best way to go.

"I'm cumming, baby! I'm cumming all over your dick!" I screamed as I had the biggest orgasm of my life.

I was satisfied and done, but Delonte's dick grew harder and he dove into me deeper. I looked up at him as sweat fell from his face onto mine. His eyes rolled up into his head and I felt him getting ready to explode.

He put the gun down on the bed, placed his hands on the top of my head and pushed me down into every stroke he made. I felt his dick all the way in my stomach and I knew it would be a matter of seconds before he'd be done.

"Oh shit I'm cumming baby ... I'm cumming!" he cried.

He pulled his dick out and busted all over my stomach. I moaned and rubbed it into my flat stomach as if it were lotion. He smiled at me, wiped the sweat from his head and licked his lips.

"Damn you got some good-ass pussy, girl."

"I know." I smiled thinking to myself, *Why couldn't I be enough?*

He laughed as he realized what I said was true. I was smiling until I noticed the expression on his face had changed after his head turned toward the left. I looked, too, and saw Kelsi standing at the doorway.

■■ ■ ■■ ■ ■■ ■ ■■

Kelsi
Chapter 14
September 25
Sunday, 10:40 pm

■■ ■ ■■ ■ ■■ ■ ■■

I had on way too much shit to be committing a murder, but it was cold outside and I was trying to dress for the occasion although my body pumped heat from the adrenaline. I was waiting on my Moms to come through with Delonte. We'd decided that after the murder, Fort Dupont in Washington D.C. was the best place to dump his lifeless body. I replayed over and over the last time I had a conversation alone with Delonte. This fool actually tried to play me.

I was ready, even though she was more than willing to pull the trigger if she had to. Still, I wanted to be the one to do it. After all, I already had a body on me and there was no need to split them up between the two of us. As I waited in the park for them to pull up, the sounds of the forest had me more uncomfortable than the deed of murdering Delonte. Fort Dupont was supposed to be a tourist attraction for hopeless out-of-towners and unsuspecting victims, but not at night. At night, you couldn't see your hand in front of your face unless a traffic light was behind you or near you. At night, crickets, grasshoppers and all other kinds of shit ruled the park like we ruled our hood.

I was there for thirty minutes before spotting the headlights. I knew it was Delonte's truck, because I hated when I was outside at home and I spotted them pulling up at the complex. I was good with spotting headlights because Moms reminded me constantly that when I drove, I had to make sure no one was following me. So I became a master at that shit.

As agreed, I let the truck pass me, and I ducked all the way down in the seat of the rental car. We agreed on 15 minutes before I would approach them. Moms said she wanted him to be calm and that would be enough time for her to do what needed to be done. I didn't want to even think about what that meant, but I had an idea. Although I was eager to get it over with, I needed a few more minutes to amp myself up, but the minutes moved like seconds.

I looked at the car radio and saw that the time was near. I wondered if Delonte told his mother he loved her. He probably did. I hoped so. Why did he have to be a snitch? Why didn't he mind his fuckin' business?! He brought this all on himself. We ain't murderers, we're fuckin' survivors! Three minutes left! Shit! "I can do this! I can fucking do this!" I repeated to convince myself. I kept replaying things over and over to make shit easier for me.

See, the first murder was easy, it was either me or him. But this was planned and plans can fuck up! I think my Moms being here also made shit a little more difficult. What if she caught a stray or something? I'd lose it! I wouldn't be no more fuckin' good. But takin' him out needed to be done, and getting myself to do it was even easier. I played scenes over and over in my head to make me hate him, including seeing him on top of my mother with a gun next to her on the bed.

Yeah, I saw that shit! I saw everything, too. I couldn't walk away. I didn't know if she was OK or if he was really gonna pull the trigger. She looked like she liked it but I didn't know if it was an act. I made myself watch just in case he got any ideas. I wanted to be there to handle his ass. I was sick the entire night, too!

We didn't talk about what I saw, but she knew it was on my mind as much as it was on hers. I hated when they messed around and left the door open, and after everything that happened recently, I hated it even more. I don't know if it bothered me more that she had sex with the man who was trying to blackmail me, or if it was the fact that she appeared to be liking it.

It was time. I reached inside the glove compartment and pulled out the gun that belonged to Charles. There wasn't much light coming through, with the exception of the light from the moon, so I held it up to closely examine it. I couldn't believe that I was getting ready to kill a man *again,* and within less than a month's time. But then again, Delonte wasn't a man, he was a punk.

I jumped out of the car, pulled my hoodie over my head, and approached Delonte's truck on the passenger side. Just like we had planned, Moms was sitting in the driver's seat and Delonte was in the passenger's. He jumped the moment I tapped on the window. He was frightened. He knew what time it was the moment he saw me. Everything he did to me, everything he said to me and everything he thought about me was between us. I saw it all.

He turned his head to my mother and then back at me trying to figure out what was going on. I saw him reach for his glove compartment and with all the power in me, I shattered the passenger side window and put the gun to his head.

"Don't move, muthafucka! Let's make this easy!"

Just like the bitch he was, he slid over to protect himself from getting anything on him.

"Get the fuck in the back!"

He didn't move.

"I SAID GET THE FUCK IN THE BACK SEAT, BEFORE I BLOW YOUR MUTHAFUCKIN' HEAD OFF!"

Now he moved carefully and slowly. Once he was out of the truck, I pushed him along with the nose of the gun and slammed the passenger car door closed. He opened the back door and I slid in the back seat with him, closing the door behind me.

"You OK, Ma? Any of that glass get on you?"

"I'm good, baby," she said as she winked at me while brushing a few of the remnants of glass off of her clothes.

"What the fuck is going on, Janet?" he asked as he looked in her direction.

She continued to brush the glass off of her clothes as I busied myself with the gun in my hands.

"Janet, what in the FUCK is going on?!"

Silence.

"Do you have any idea who you're fucking with? Do you know who I AM? I'm Delonte muthafuckin' Knight!!!!"

Silence.

"Do you realize what the fuck you are doing, bitch?!" he continued.

Silence.

I heard enough. He'd called my mother out of her name and that's where I drew the line. With the butt of the gun, I knocked him upside his head, and he fell against the left window. His blood made the gun slide a little in my hand but it wouldn't be the first time I felt another man's blood.

"Don't make me shoot you, Delonte, because I will. Now you're gonna shut the fuck up, and listen to what we have to say. If you don't, you're dead." My words were slow, deliberate and clear so he wouldn't miss a thing.

He looked at me like he'd seen a ghost and then back at my mother.

"Janet," he said as he stole one last look at me. "What's going on? Why are you doing this?"

Silence.

133

She was having a good time playing on his emotions. I learned from her that silence could do more damage to a man's emotional state of mind than words could ever do.

She reached into the new black Prada purse I saw her bring in yesterday, pulled out a pack of Kool menthol cigarettes and lit one. After she took her fifth puff, she turned around to face Delonte and blew the smoke in his face. I couldn't believe she was smoking. She never smoked so I figured she was getting into character.

"What am I doing?" She laughed. "What am I doing? Let's see. What I'm doing is giving you a chance to tell me where you keep your shit." She looked at him the same way I'd seen her do when she asked for money to go shopping.

"Are you kidding me?! Are you fucking kidding me?!" Spit flew out of his mouth as he yelled.

"No, Jarvis," she said as she puffed her cigarette again and blew it in his face. "I'm not kidding."

I wondered who in the fuck Jarvis was. She called him that a lot lately when she talked to me about him. I had been meaning to ask her about it.

"But baby," he said, responding to the name as if it belonged to him. He probably was so scared she could have called him Lil Kim and he would have answered to it. "I do everything for you. Why are you doing this to me?"

I kept the gun pointed firmly at him. I was ready for her at anytime to say, "Blast this muthafucka!" I was like a trained dog ready and willing to annihilate him. My hand shook and I was itching to pull the trigger just thinking about all the games he played. I started feeding myself bullshit just for kicks. *He probably fucked Keisha when you were dealin' with that nigga Charles. That's probably why she be smilin' in his face. I wouldn't be surprised if she sucked his dick. Calm down, Kelsi. You'll have your chance in a minute*, I told myself.

"Delonte, I'm gonna ask you one time and one time only. If you don't tell me what I need to know," she said as she puffed the cigarette again and then put it out in his leather seat, "I'm gonna instruct Kelsi to pull the trigger. You wouldn't want him to pull the trigger, now would you?"

I heard my mother's words but slightly. Delonte had my full attention. Any wrong move and it would be over before he realized and maybe even over before it was time. I had mentally programmed myself to be ready the moment she said my name. I didn't care about all my mother's plans even though she didn't waste any time sharing them with me either. Although it would be a shame if she said, "KELSI, let him live," because at this point, I would've just heard my name and fired.

The only thing I wanted was to get rid of this snitch and dump the body. I was sure killing him extended outside of blackmailing me and what he had done to my Moms. She had some other plans that I'm sure we'd discuss later. The image of Delonte fucking her brains out was also still fresh in my mind which made me clench the gun even tighter.

"Baby, please," he cried as tears fell down his face. "Baby, please don't do this to me, I love you. I thought you loved me and wanted to work on our relationship."

She laughed and shook her head. "Delonte, if you say that bullshit again I'm gonna use this blade in my purse to slice your throat. Do you understand me? Now, are you going to tell me or not?"

She was cold and her mannerisms were similar to the female gangstas I'd seen on TV. I was trying to determine if she was acting because it all came too easy. She cared less about his crocodile tears than I did. I wondered what was going on in his mind. I wondered if he realized that everything was over for him. I wondered if he knew he'd cashed in his last ticket in life and it was a loser.

"Do you understand me, muthafucka?!" she asked again.

He nodded his head yes.

"Before I tell you, can I ask why you're doing this baby? Please."

She laughed and dug in her purse to reapply her lip-gloss to freshen up using the rearview mirror.

"Do you realize I got my hair cut short for you?"

"What?" he intoned in a low voice.

"I said, do you realize that I cut my hair short for you?" she repeated.

"No I didn't, but I like it."

"Well, the day I wore it short, you didn't even notice. I think you said something like, 'You look different, but I don't know what it is.' I can't really remember what you said actually, and you know why I can't remember?"

"Because I wasn't paying enough attention to you and you forgot?" he answered, taking a shot in the dark.

"No! I can't remember because I realize I really didn't give a fuck. I didn't give a fuck about YOU or this weak-ass relationship. I thought I did, but I didn't. The only thing I gave a fuck about was Kelsi and the dollas, baby."

"Why are you doing this?!" he cried, uncertain of his future.

I laughed inside, loving the mental game she was playing with him. Here it was, his life dangled in the wind, and she was putting on MAC and asking him miscellaneous bullshit-ass questions.

"*Well* ... let's see. Why am I doing this?" she repeated as she smiled at herself in the mirror before turning around to smile at me. "I'm doing this because you tried to blackmail my son." I wondered if he would mention the details of the blackmail because I still hadn't told her I sold drugs. As far as she was concerned, murder was my first crime and it was done in self-defense. She stuffed the makeup in her purse and turned around to look at him. "I'm doing this because you've cheated on me ever since we've been together. I'm doing this because I'm tired of living check to check. Hold up, I don't have a check anymore, remember, I quit my jobs. I'm doing this because you've wasted my time, and I'm doing this because it's time for me to get paid."

"But –"

"J, when you gonna quit your job? I need you," she interrupted, mimicking him. "Yeah, you need me all right, but right now, I need to get paid and you the muthafuckin' jackpot." She nodded her head as if she were satisfied with the answer she had given him.

"Now," she said as she placed her hand on his face as if she were concerned. "Where do you keep your money and the weight?"

Before she let him answer, she placed her index finger over his lips as if to hush him. "Let me remind you, if you give me any other answer besides the one *I want to hear*, you're dead. Do you understand me?"

Again, he nodded his head yes.

Delonte wiped his face with his hands, and rubbed them on his jeans. Here in the back of his truck, he resembled a scared little girl more than he did a grown-ass man. I could tell he was contemplating whether or not to tell her anything. His thought process lasted all of 10 seconds when he realized his life was on the line.

"OK, OK, baby," he stuttered. "Ummm, I keep most of the weight at my Moms'. Kenosha knows where it is because she helps me separate it. If you don't believe me you can call her right now," he continued while looking at me and then back at my Moms like he was trying to convince us both. "But Janet, you need to know some things, too."

"The only thing I need to know is where you keep the

muthafuckin' money! That's it!"

"It's about Skully."

"Like I said, the only thing I want to hear is about the money and weight!"

"OK ... Umm, OK, ummmm, I keep some money there, too, and the rest is in my truck under the front seat."

Keeping her eyes on Delonte, Moms ran her hand under the seat and pulled out two stacks of money and kissed them both. She tucked one in her purse and the other in her shirt because both wouldn't fit inside the bag.

"There you go, baby," she crooned as if it were all over. "Was that so hard? You acted like it was so difficult. You did it! It's all over now."

She smiled trying to convince him it was all over, and you know what that punk did? He smiled back as if the worst was over. I further realized that Delonte ain't have no business in the game because his heart was weak. Did he actually think we would rob him, let him live and look behind our backs for the rest of our lives? He was grimey, untrustworthy and a snake. So even if he said he'd leave us alone, his word couldn't be trusted. He had to go. Bottom line. End of Story.

"Now you wouldn't happen to be lying to me now would you?" she asked, narrowing her eyes.

"Baby, no!! I swear I'm not!" he cried as he shook his head no. "You can trust me."

My mother looked at me when he said that. She always told me that when a man says you can trust him, you can't. If he *can* be trusted, you'll know it, and the words would never have to be spoken.

"Where them shirts at? The ones with the blood on 'em?" I asked, remembering he still had them.

"They're at my mother's house, too. I swear!" He was breathing hard and sweating profusely. "Kelsi, I'm so sorry for blackmailing you, man. For real. This shit will never happen again. You'll see, Kelsi!"

I held the gun firmly toward him, nodded my head a little to the right and gave him less than a half of a smile.

"Yeah, I know. I know man."

I wasn't lying. I did know. None of this shit would ever happen again.

My mother grabbed Delonte's piece in the glove compartment, got out of the car, looked down the dark road and opened Delonte's door. A few cars had driven by but none of them noticed us. The crickets were loud as hell and every bug in the entire park seemed to be right outside the door … eavesdropping. I'm a city nigga for real, so the sounds had me vexed.

She nodded at me, which meant get ready. She moved toward Delonte, kissed him and said, "Damn, I'm gonna miss you."

His eyes grew three times bigger and he pushed her to the side and tried to run. A nigga running for his life is the hardest nigga to catch. The only nigga that can catch him is another nigga running for his life. See, I was the one he had the drop on. There was no way on earth I was letting this snitchin'-ass snake get away from me.

When she looked at me I heard the words I'd been waiting on.

"KELSI! NOWWW!"

I was already out of the truck and then I did it. He was runnin' fast as a muthafucka. I had to give him credit for that, but every nigga knows you can't run faster than the bullets in a gun.

COCK … CLICK … BOOM! BOOM! BOOM!

He fell down and I walked up on him. I wanted to be sure. I needed to be sure.

I shot him again, point blank as his body lay motionless on the ground. I stuffed the gun in my pocket and pulled his body toward the woods. I was hyped and moved quick! All I needed was a car comin' down the road and seein' me haulin' his ass.

In the darkness, I made my way through the woods with my mother shining a flashlight behind me. She was also holding the shovel I packed earlier. When I figured we'd gone far enough, I started digging a hole big enough to bury his body. Spiderwebs, snakes, and all other kinds of shit were surrounding us. Burying his body out here would make him right at home. I was tryin' to move quickly because this nature shit made me a little uncomfortable. But a nervous nigga made too many mistakes and I wasn't trying to make any of those.

Hot, sweaty and amped, I emptied his pockets and threw him in the hole which would now be his new home. I looked back at my mother once, but she didn't look like herself. She was smiling more and appeared to enjoy what we were doing.

"He can't bother you now, baby," she said looking up at me. "He can't take my baby away from me now."

I was happy she was at ease instead of nervous or frightened. Good. I'd rather she be OK with it than be fucked up about it later. There in the semi-darkness, she took pride in every pile of dirt I threw on his face. We were covering our skeletons together. Delonte's death would be a secret we would take to our grave, and my mother is the only person in the world I knew I could trust with it.

When it was over, we walked back to the truck after making sure the coast was clear. Before I got back into the rental car, we sat in Delonte's truck in silence. After five minutes, we looked at each other and smiled. She told me not to worry and that she had everything else under control. Apparently, she was taking his truck somewhere where it would be no more. Where did she have these connections? I wanted to protect my mother but here she was protecting me.

She placed her hand on my leg and said, "Baby, life as you

know it has changed for us. Sometimes you got to take what the fuck you want. Be careful of greed. See, Delonte was greedy and he had this comin'. But remember, no matter what happens with everybody else, you will always be my soldier and once again tonight, you proved it. It's time to start living like we used to. Are you ready to claim what's rightfully ours?"

"Yes," I answered, not knowing what I was agreeing to.

"Good. Because you were too young to remember but trust me, you had everything, and I don't want you to ever have to want for anything again. I'll take care of everything, Kelsi. You're a hustler's son!" she said as tears streamed down her face.

I smiled at her and said, "As long as I have you, I will never want for nothing."

Kelsi
Chapter 15
September 28
Wednesday, 4:30 pm

It had been three days since we killed Delonte. Kenosha and his mother were taking it bad. They didn't find the body, but they knew something was up. I felt some kind of way about it, but it was only because I wasn't trying to hurt them. Don't get me wrong, I ain't have no remorse for what I did, but I hated to see people's mothers cry. Delonte's mother cried every time she came over. Her crying reminded me of what we'd done and I'd make up an excuse to leave. I kept thinking about my mother and how she would feel if something happened to me. I hated to see my mother in pain, but my regret for killing Delonte ended at his mother's pain. In my heart, he deserved exactly what the fuck he got.

Mrs. Knight's house smelled liked somethin' was cooking all the time, even though it wasn't. I had only been in the house for ten minutes and already I was hungry. Kenosha made me some fried bologna sandwiches but I was kinda hoping that Mrs. Knight would get in the kitchen and make it happen. With Delonte missin', I could forget about that shit. I was there because Kenosha called the house about fifty times looking for Delonte. When I finally answered she was out in front of my house to swoop me up.

To make her feel better, as if that were possible, I offered to take a ride with her. The next thing I knew, we ended up over at her house on Clay. It worked out just right because when Delonte told us where he kept his money and his weight, I had planned on getting into the house by any means necessary. I suggested we stop by Mrs. Knight's house, which was a few doors down, to say hello.

"Where Mrs. Knight go?" I asked as I drank the lemon lime Kool-Aid she poured for me.

"She's going to church to pray for Delonte," she said as she broke down in tears and sat next to me on the couch. "Kelsi, what I'm gonna do? I ain't got nobody that look out for me like Delonte. I ain't got shit, Kelsi."

I put the cup down, slid next to her and wrapped my arms around her. The moment I did, she fell into me.

"I'll look out for you," I said, not knowing where that came from.

Niggas got in trouble for making promises to chicks they ain't have no intentions on keeping, but I needed to get into Delonte's room. I was willing to sell her some more shit if she'd buy it.

"Boooyee, stop playyin wit me. Don't make promises you can't keep."

"I'm serious, girl."

I held her close because I knew girls liked that shit. For five minutes, Kenosha went on and on about shit I ain't feel like hearing. I mean, I ain't give a fuck about none of that shit he used to do for her. None of it. In my opinion he was a bum and the world was better off without him.

While she was in her own world, I scanned the house with my eyes. I gave her an occasional nod to make her think I was listening. All I saw was a bunch of dumb-ass pictures of Delonte as a kid. When I saw the one of him and Mrs. Knight,

I felt uncomfortable, *again*. Mrs. Knight held Delonte in her arms, as a baby. I thought about how my Moms would feel if somethin' fucked up happened to me. That's probably why she was pressin' the issue to bury his ass. Right when I felt a little weird, Kenosha ran her hand in between my legs.

"Whoa!" I let out.

"What."

Silence.

What was she doing? Gramps was upstairs in his room and although Mrs. Knight had just walked out the door, there was no telling when she'd be back. Plus, I wasn't tryin' to fuck Kenosha in Delonte's house. I was cruddy but not that cruddy. There was a plan and I had to stick to it. I was there for the product and the loot, not to bang Kenosha's back out. Although for real, I'd have loved to kill two birds with one stone.

"Kenosha, don't worry about shit, Delonte's gonna show up. Trust me," I said as I held the hand she had between my legs. "You getting all worked up over nothing."

She sat up, wiped the tears from her face and said, "Kelseee, how old you is now?"

"I'm 15, but I'll be 16 next month. Why?"

"Cuz you real cool. Your girl real lucky. I mean, you act older than most of the men my age."

I wasn't trying to fall for Kenosha's games, but my chest was on swole for a minute. I mean, she was 25 or somethin' and here she was feelin' me. Any other time I'd have my dick in her ass for bragging rights alone. But right now, there was a job to be done – finding out where Delonte kept his shit. I needed to think of something. I wished there were really a thinking cap, because I needed that muthafucka. I wondered if he was lying or if he really kept his shit there. It's not like it wouldn't be a good place. Nobody would suspect drugs and loot in this old-ass house unless a drug dealer lived here, in which he didn't.

A Hustler's Son

I ain't never been inside Delonte's house so I had no idea of the set up. The closest I got to his place was the front porch and he never invited me in. I should've known then that he ain't fuck with me. I knew he had a room somewhere in the house, and I figured what I was looking for would be in there somewhere. I had to think of a way to get from up under Kenosha.

"Kenosha, where's the bathroom?"

"What you gonna do Kelseeee, number one or two?"

"Girl, stop playing. Where the bathroom at?"

"I'm just playin', boyyee. It's at the top of the stairs to the left. But don't be dropping no stupid loads for real! And only use a lil' bit of toilet paper. It can stop up the toilet."

I jumped up and made my way to the bathroom. Once upstairs, I peeped the layout. The bathroom was the first door I came to and the bedrooms were next. I looked downstairs and noticed that as long as Kenosha kept her ass on the couch, she wouldn't be able to see me, or what I was doing.

I opened the bathroom door and ran the water in the sink, then closed it behind me. I wanted her to think I was doing whatever in the bathroom and not in the rest of the house.

Slowly and carefully I moved toward his room. I knew which one it was because it said "Delonte's Room" on the door. I shook my head and laughed that a man his age had a sign on his door. I mean, I'm a teenager and I wouldn't be caught dead with that shit on my door.

When I opened the door to his room, the same cologne smell I hated filled the air. It was so strong that it smelled like the bottle was broken. When I looked around the room again, I noticed everything was out of place. Who in the fuck been in here? There was enough light from the window, so I could definitely see what was going on. Somebody had beaten me to Delonte's room! Shit! Everything was everywhere but where it needed to be.

Still, I had to check. There was no way I'd tell my mother I got an easy ride to Delonte's house and didn't look for anything. So I looked on the dresser, under the bed, in his closet and even on the floor. I wasn't tryin' to make too much noise although I doubted anybody could hear me since Gramps was snoring like a bear in the room next door. I was pushing shit over with my feet and trying to make my way through the mess. I wasn't sure, but somethin' told me I wasn't findin' no weight or money in this room, let alone this house.

Somebody fucked his room up good! I mean, all of his stuff was knocked off the dresser and most of the stuff was on his bed and the floor. I was getting ready to give up and turn around, until I saw Kenosha standing behind me. Her tiny waist and round hips almost turned me on until I realized I wasn't supposed to be in that muthafucka.

"What you doin', boy? Why you in my cuzzin's room?"

Shit! I was so pressed trying to find his shit that I was caught slippin'. I had to think of something quick.

"Girl, don't play wit me. You know what the fuck is up," I said, giving my best Denzel Washington impression that I could.

"No, Kelsee. I *don't*," she said with an attitude. "Now what the fuck you doin' in my cuzzin's room?" she asked with her hands on her hips. "Somethin' lookin real *conspi-shious* around here and I don't like it! So what the fuck is goin on, *Kelllssee*?!"

"Fuck that shit you tell me!" I was giving it to her hard. "You down there playin' games, feelin' on my dick and shit, what the fuck you think I'm doin' in here? I'm lookin' for a rubber so we can handle business. Unless you scared."

Her expression changed from, "I know you ain't sneakin' in my cuzzin's room" to "Oooo Kelsee, for real?"

She licked her lips, looked me up and down and said, "Well did you find what you were looking for?"

Since she bought that shit, I tried to sell her something else, too. I figured I would hint around to finding out who'd been in his room so I said, "Naw, I ain't find shit in this muthafucka! I can't believe he kept his shit like this. His drawers were on the floor."

She laughed and pushed me toward the bed. I moved some of that shit on the floor and got settled. With my legs hanging off the edge and my back up against the wall, she straddled me in the sitting position.

"Boyeee, Delonte ain't leave his room like this, my grandmother did. She was trying to find some info 'bout where he may be, but she found something else instead and like to lost her mind."

Kenosha ain't have to say shit else because I knew what she found. Delonte's stash. My only question now was what did she do with it? But how was I gonna ask Kenosha? I ain't have no business over there and I ain't have no business lookin' for his shit. But that didn't help the fact that I wanted to know.

Fuck it! I thought. I'd ask her anyway.

"Straight up?!" I said, fake surprised. "What she find?" I asked as I squeezed her ass and moved into her. *Damn!* That felt good, too.

She looked at me and kissed me. "She found," *kiss* "something," *kiss kiss,* "that she shouldn't have found." *Kiss kiss.*

I knew it! Mrs. Knight found Delonte's shit and got it the fuck out her house. She lived in D.C. long enough to know that the government ain't have no mercy just because you old. They would have dragged Mr. and Mrs. Knight's asses straight to jail if they raided this place. Shit! It was almost a complete waste of time to be over there, until I looked at how sexy Kenosha looked on top of me. I might as well make the best of it.

"You soft as shit," I moaned as I grabbed her fat ass, pulling her down to grind on my dick.

"And you're hard." She laughed.

"You got a condom?" I asked as I smiled at her.

"You know *iiiiitttt,*" she said as she winked at me, reached in her bra, and pulled one out.

"Damn, Kenosha. It's like that?!"

"Boy, I knew I was fuckin' you the moment you got in my car. It ain't but one thing that gets my mind off of stuff and talkin' ain't it."

"Is that right?"

"Yes, that's right."

"I thought you wanted me here to chill with you. You know, cuz Delonte missing and shit."

"I do, but the best way to get over shit is by fucking."

"I'm wit it."

This girl was a freak, but damn was she sexy. With the corner of her teeth she tore off the edge of the condom and spit it out. With the half opened pack dangling in her mouth, she unzipped my pants, pulled my dick out of my boxers, and slid it on.

Then for some reason, my mother popped in my head. *Never use their condoms, Kelsi. Trust me. Them fast-ass little girls will try to set you up and get pregnant. Always carry your own shit.* When I remembered that, I had all intentions of telling shawty it was no haps, but before I got to do that, she was getting into position. As she lifted her waist and slid down on me, I thought to myself, *What mama don't know won't hurt her.*

A Hustler's Son

Tryin' not to blow up about every little thing was becoming harder to do. I had come to realize that I was a perfectionist, and with perfection comes stress. I wanted the murder to be done smoothly, his money to be collected and for us to move on with our lives. But it wasn't working like that. I realized this is what happened in this lifestyle but it didn't make things any easier.

It didn't help that Kelsi called to tell me that he was with Kenosha. These little girls just wouldn't leave my baby alone. Don't get me wrong, I was happy he had an easy way into Delonte's house, even though he ain't find shit, but I *despised* her ass. I didn't want that bitch to have the hold on Kelsi that she had on Delonte. She was sneaky and underhanded. I'd just as soon walk him down the aisle with Lakeisha before I'd see him with Kenosha.

If she had met two other niggas, I wouldn't care. I may have even respected her game or liked her. But she was trying to use sex to hold her own cousin, my man and now my son. I wouldn't be surprised if she had her eyes on Kelsi for the longest. I mean, my baby is handsome but don't nothing about his mind or his body say 15 anything, besides the love he had for me. I hoped that would never change.

"OK, Kelsi, but what I tell you about talking about this kind of stuff on the home phone?"

"I know, Ma, I just wanted you to know what was up."

Click Click. That was the third time the other line had beeped since I'd been talking to Kelsi and each time it was Keisha. These bitches were driving me crazy around here.

"Look Kelsi, the other line's for me. I'll talk to you later, baby." I clicked on the other line.

"Hello?"

"Hello?"

"Yes?" I said as I plopped on the couch and propped the phone on my shoulder so I could free my hands to remove my shoes.

"Hi Ms. Stayley, is Kelsi there?"

I could've said no, but I thought of a plan to rid Kelsi of Lakeisha. No matter what the age, no woman liked her man keeping time with another bitch, especially a bitch named Kenosha. So in my fakest and friendliest voice I could find I said, "Hey baby. How are you?"

The moment my words came out, I immediately wanted to throw up. But I'm an actress first, *always*.

"Uh, Mrs. Stayley, this is uh Keisha," she responded, shocked by my tone of voice. It was then that I realized that she was aware I couldn't stand her ass, too.

"I know, honey." I giggled. "I can't ask how you're doing?"

"Uh … yes. I'm fine Ms. Stayley."

"Great! What's going on?"

"I've been lookin' for Kelsi. Is he home?"

"No," I said as if I didn't want to break her heart. "But you're welcome to call him on his cell phone. Do you have the number?"

"Yes, but he ain't answerin'."

"Baby, I want to tell you something. You know, woman to

woman."

"Sure Ms. Stayley!" She thought this sista-girl moment was the perfect opportunity to pick the mother of her boyfriend's mind. "What is it?"

"First things first, call me Janet."

"OK," she said, shocked by my request because I had told that little bitch the next time she called me Janet I would be dragging her ass by the hair, and out of my house for good! But that was then.

"Secondly, what I'm about to tell you, I'm telling you because I like you. If it ever gets back to Kelsi that I told you, I won't have any respect for you, and you won't be allowed to call or come over here ever again. Do you understand?"

"Yes, Ms. Stayley," she responded in between heavy breaths. "But I'm scared. I'm not sure I want to hear this."

"I know you are, honey, but this is all a part of being a woman. You have to hear certain things and be able to take 'em, even though you don't want to. Think of me as your big sister and your friend. Sometimes you have to hear things you don't want to, in order to make the right decisions for yourself. You understand?"

"I understand, Ms. Stayley, I mean, Janet," she said as she started crying.

This was sickening. What the fuck was she crying about? I hadn't even told her anything yet. I already knew now that she was going to be out of the picture no matter what I did. So as far as I was concerned, I was just helping the process along and the more she showed she ain't have heart, the more I hated her guts. My son was getting ready to sit on an empire, and her weak ass would probably get him killed.

"Well Keisha, it's like this. Kelsi ain't here cuz he's with Kenosha. I don't know if you realize it, but they've been spending a lot of time together. You may have to consider moving on.

I told Kelsi ya'll to young anyway to be in a relationship." I stopped after realizing my true feelings about this bitch were starting to seep out again, so I had to play it off. "But when I met you, and got to know you even more, I thought you were perfect for him. This is why I'm telling you what's going on between Kenosha and Kelsi. They're acting like they're in love. You may have even seen them together lately. Have you?"

At this time she was crying so hard that I didn't know if she was able to hear anything I said outside of Kelsi being with Kenosha.

"Uh, yes I have seen her around him, just the other day actually. Ms. Janet, I mean, Janet, what I'm gonna do without Kelsi? I don't have no life without him."

"What are you gonna do? A lot of things! For starters you can make his ass come to you by not calling him or taking his shit. I mean he's my son and all, but he's still a man who *needs* to be put in his place."

"Put in his place?" she repeated in between sniffling.

"Yes. Make him want you … just as much as you want him."

I thought about what I was telling her for a minute, and I decided that if anyone was feeding me half of the shit I was feeding her, I would have known what was up. But like I said, Keisha ain't have no heart so she believed *everything* I said. After all, why would I lie? I was his mother.

"You right, Janet. I'm not saying shit to Kelsi until he does right by me. He'll call me before I'll call him!"

"That's right, girl, but be careful about the time you put on it. A man hasn't been fully broken down until you hold back on the pussy, stop calling, start dating new people and leave him alone for at least two months."

"Oh no, Ms. Stayley, Kelsi and I aren't sleeping with each other."

"Keisha please. I just confided in you and you're going to

lie to me? I know you and K-man fuckin'. Hell, I told him how to put on a condom. Plus, you be at my house every weekend. Do you think I'm that stupid?"

She was silent before she said, "You're right, Janet. I wasn't tryin' to lie to you, it's just kinda of embarrassin' that's all."

"Well we have to be real with each other, Lakeisha."

"You're right. And I'm gonna take your advice starting today. Don't bother telling Kelsi I called cuz I'm gonna give him a taste of his own medicine."

"Good idea, Keisha. Hey, what you think about Bricks?"

"What you mean, Janet?"

"What do you think about him?"

"Nothin!" she shot back. "He's Kelsi's best friend."

"Listen to me. What I'm about to tell you may save you and Kelsi's relationship," I said in a low voice. "It's actually one of the oldest tricks in the book."

Her ear was so close to the phone that at one point I could have sworn I felt it.

"A man is weak when it comes to his best friend and his girlfriend. Maybe hanging around him a little will give Kelsi a taste of his own medicine."

"I don't know about that, Mrs. Stayley, I mean Mrs. Janet, I mean Janet," she said, nervous by the idea.

"Trust me. Spending time with your man's best friend is the best way to get even. Now I'm not saying sleep with him, just spend time with him. Now you can't let Bricks know what you're doing. I have a feeling about him and if I'm right, he won't appreciate what you're doing. When you talk to him, tell him you're trying to find out what's going on with Kelsi and why he won't talk to you. Don't let him know he's a part of your plan to get back at him."

"You sure about this, Janet?" she asked in a hesitated tone.

"Yes."

"If you really think it will work."

"I know it will, Keisha."

"OK, I'll do it. Thanks for being honest with me, Janet. I really appreciate everything you're doing for me."

"No problem, sweetheart. Us girls have to stick together. Bye."

"Bye."

When she hung up, I walked to the kitchen and poured myself a glass of Grey Goose straight up, no ice. That chile is a complete idiot! I hated what I was doing to Kelsi by ridding him of Keisha, but we had too much shit going on to have any outside influences fuck anything up. One wrong person in our circle could mean our lives, and I'd die without Kelsi. If Keisha were sharp, I'd have allowed him to keep her, but look how easy it was for her to buy into the nonsense I fed her. Look how easy it was for her to talk to the cops and give info on her own boyfriend. She was too naive and she couldn't be on Kelsi's arm if I had anything to do with it, and I did!

Besides, after killing Jarvis, I mean, Delonte, I made preparations to move the weight I knew he had with some connections I made from working at the hotel. A lot of big time dealers ran through there and most of them wanted ass and my number. I did what I wanted to do on the side, but for real I was keeping numbers just in case I reentered the game, and I was glad I did. I duplicated the list and gave the other to Kelsi. I never knew when it might be valuable to him.

Now that Kelsi told me he couldn't find anything in Delonte's house, I ain't know what my next move would be. I knew whatever I wanted to do now, I needed dough to do it. Hell, I had over twenty grand in the past two weeks, which is more than I would have made in a year as a housekeeper, and already I wanted more. I had even contacted the man who saved my life five years ago because I knew he dealt in big weight.

With the money I made from my connects, I was gonna flip it with him, but now I ain't have shit.

Hating how my clothes felt against my body, I took off the shirt I was wearing. When I did, I accidentally rubbed my hand over the wounds where the gunshots entered and exited my body, a constant reminder of my ex-boyfriend, Jarvis. I was reminded then of my own greed and passion. I always lied to Kelsi about my wounds, never wanting to reveal their awful past. I should have ignored all further urges to get into the life again, but instead, I looked at my wounds as a reminder of what *not* to do next time.

Even though it happened years ago, I could remember every word they spoke while I lay hidden in the back of a stranger's car.

Five Years Ago

"What up man. Where you goin'?" Jarvis asked as he approached the man who saved me, and stood directly behind the truck that concealed my bullet-ridden body. Their voices were so close, I could tell that all they had to do was glance in the window of the truck and they'd see me.

"Who the fuck you talking to?! Don't fuckin' ask me no questions!" The one who saved me yelled.

"It's cool, I'm just fuckin' with you. We were supposed to be meeting you in the building but you weren't there," Jarvis responded.

"Yeah. I was out here handling other business. So what's up? You got my shit?"

"Look, we got it but we have to take care of some other stuff first. We ain't want you thinking we were bullshitting," Jarvis said.

"Well, I think you are bullshitting me, nigga. You betta not be fuckin' around with my cash again. Not even Kyope would

stop me from the shit I'd do to you!"

"Easy man. I thought that shit was squashed." Jarvis was playing and I could tell it was pissing him off.

"Stop playin' with me, nigga! I'm not your bitch! You tell me to meet you here, and you ain't got my money or my product. Don't fuck with me, Jarvis, cuz I ain't in the playin' mood."

I lay there under the blankets, barely moving for fear that they would see me, for fear that some shit was getting ready to kick off, and all of my chances of goin' home would be lost. It would be like winning a million dollars and having it taken away. I needed to go home but anything could happen now. Jarvis could rob him, take the truck, find me in the back and succeed at finishing what he started, killing me. Or a stray bullet could hit me and I could bleed to death. Bleed. I was already bleeding. I bent my chin down and saw my blood all over the place. I know just as much was outside as it was inside. I wondered how far my blood trail reached before the one who saved me put me in the truck.

Still, I was amazed at how he managed to put Jarvis in his place. Maybe Jarvis feared him and didn't want no beef, because it was unlike him to take the back seat while niggas gave it to him. Jarvis always had the upper hand and at times, he was hot tempered.

He once killed a waiter at our favorite restaurant because he brought him the check without Jarvis asking him to. He told me it was embarrassing because bringing the check earlier made him feel that his business wasn't any good. I agreed in his presence, although I didn't feel that way in my heart.

"I ain't fuckin with you." I could sense in Jarvis' voice that he reached the limit. I was afraid of what might happen next. It was obvious that the strange man didn't like Jarvis and Jarvis ain't care for him either. There was silence for a minute and then Jarvis said, "You right, man. I got some shit I got to do real

quick but all your shit will be here before you slide back to Maryland. Let us take care of wha –"

He interrupted Jarvis. "I need another excuse like I need another asshole. Bring my shit tomorrow night, same time, same place."

Without waiting for a response, he jumped in the truck and we drove off.

For the first time since he put me in his truck, I took a deep breath and passed out.

**Janet
Chapter 17
September 28
Wednesday, 7:45 pm**

I had too many people around me who weren't down for me like I was down for them. I was determined not to make the same mistake twice or allow any outside influences in our lives that could possibly ruin things for us. I already began to clean the slate starting with Jarvis, I mean Delonte. Next it would be Lakeisha and then Bricks if I had to. In my mind, anybody in the way would be a target, therefore they had to be eliminated.

I walked over to the couch with a drink in my hand and grabbed my cell phone. I needed to call the one who saved me five years back because he was waiting on my call, then I remembered what Delonte said before he took his last breath. "I have to tell you some things. It's about Skully." I quickly put them out of my mind because scared men told many lies.

All I was thinking about now was the call that needed to be made. I told him I would give him any weight and money I had from Delonte in exchange for a larger load, but here I was, calling him to say I couldn't come through. My phone call would appear as if I weren't capable, even though I knew I was. I had secret medals all on my jacket from the work I put in over the years. Still, coming to him empty-handed was unprofessional and worthless, but telling him nothing was even worse. I took two deep breaths before making the call. One … two.

"Hey, it's me, I couldn't find shit."

"Where you callin' me from?" he asked directly, which sent shivers down my spine.

He wasn't much on introductions, so I made sure not to give him any.

"My cell," I answered with the same serious tone.

"I thought you said it was a sure thing. I thought you said you knew exactly where the shit was."

"I did, but somebody who shouldn't have, found it. I got 15 right now, you think I can get a key?"

"J, why you doing this?"

"Because I'm tired of my son living around here. Plus, shit's getting hot for us."

"You better be sure before crossing this line with me. I mean, right now we're cool. Outside of doing a favor or two for you, we don't really interact but if you fuck with my money or me, I'll kill you. Do you understand what I'm saying?"

I thought about his question carefully before answering, knowing once I got in, there was no turning back. "I understand and I won't fuck with your shit cuz I know you. I would have never come to you unless I was ready. I ain't no stranger to this lifestyle," I reminded him then downed the rest of my drink.

"Yeah but you a stranger to this lifestyle with me. I'm telling you that although I saved your ass from Jarvis that night, if you cross me, I'll act like I never knew you. So again … are you sure?"

"Yes." This time I didn't hesitate. It was all about Kelsi.

"Why you wanna do this?"

"You know what Jarvis told me the night he was about to kill me? He told me *Nobody has heart when they're dead.* That was his response the night he was gonna kill me because I told him that even if I died, I'd still have more heart than him."

"Like I said, why are you doing this?"

"Because I believe you don't pick the life you lead, it picks you. I'm a hustler, and I always will be. Wearing a waitress or housekeeping uniform didn't change shit. So when Jarvis told me 'you don't have heart when you're dead,' I told him that was bullshit because the soul lives on! If I have enough heart to take a man's life, and to protect mine at all costs, unlike his punk ass, who was willing to give me up to save himself, I believe that I'll have the same heart when I'm six feet deep!"

"But why the FUCK are you doing this, Janet? Everything is OK now," he said as if he didn't hear anything I had to say.

"Because OK's for regular people … I'm not regular. I fuckin' love the streets. It's all I know."

"You don't want this with me. So I'm gonna ask you one last time, why are you doing this?"

"No, you tell me why you saved me!" I sounded a little bolder than I should have but this was a question that I had been wanting to ask for years. Not only was this man the only reason I'm breathing now, but he was the most vicious muthafucka I knew. He didn't have to hide me that night in New York when Jarvis tried to kill me. So why was I here? Whenever I asked him in the past, he'd avoid the question.

"I don't answer muthafuckin' questions, I ask them."

"Well I want you to answer this for me! Please."

Silence.

"I ain't tryin' to disrespect you. You know that, but I believe you saved me because although I told you they were tryin' to kill me because I helped set up Kyope, you knew I had heart, and you knew that one day, you could possibly use me. You saw the honor and the code of the streets all over me. I'm ready now! Not tomorrow, not yesterday, but now! All I'm askin' is for you to give me a chance. Put me back out there so I can take care of my son and give him what he deserves. I'm tired of workin' these nine to fives for nothin'. Please."

He was silent for five seconds before sayin, "Get more cake and then we can talk. That's how I'll know you're really ready." He hung up.

I smiled because I realized that I was finally right about him. He was about to put me out there because he knew I was ready. In the past, he was always so secretive and every time I thought I knew him, I found out I didn't. Like when we first came to The Woods, I thought he would at least make sure we had food and furniture. He knew I ain't have money to buy shit but he let me and my son lay on that floor until Delonte came. Four months later, I opened the mail and there was a strange-looking envelope amongst all the other shit. I carefully opened it and inside was three thousand dollars with a note sayin', *"I help those who help themselves."* I guess getting a job showed him I wasn't dependent, but independent. I knew then that he was deeper than I thought.

When the phone rang I lifted it to look at the caller ID and put it back down when I saw it was Delonte's mother, *again.* She'd been calling every day bothering me about where Delonte was and if I had heard from him. She thought I had something to do with his disappearance and felt by calling me every day, she'd break me down. Yeah right! I was beaten, shot, raped, framed and thrown in the trunk of a car. Surely I could take a few phone calls from his wretched-ass mother.

I was lying up against the sofa, trying to get comfortable when I heard three aggressive knocks at the door. The knocks sounded different from any I'd ever heard on this door before, but not different from knocks I've heard in the past. They sounded like whoever was doing it felt they had the authority to. Damn! The cops!

Shit! I was pacing the floor trying to think. I sat down when I realized it wasn't helping. If I didn't answer it, they were gonna keep coming back. They probably already ran the plates on every car out front, including the Acura I just bought at the auction with temporaries on it. They knew that I was here. The knock was loud enough to wake me if I were sleeping. It was steady enough that I could hear it in the shower through the running water, so not answering it wouldn't work.

I ran to the counter, reached in my purse and grabbed a piece of gum. I was chewing it for blood. Shit! Shit! Shit! I forgot that gum only intensifies the smell of alcohol but what was I worried about? I'm at home! Some things I learned in the streets were starting to come back when I didn't need them to. There's one thing I'd never forget, no matter how much time passed, and that was the law. I brushed myself off, took two deep breaths and calmed down.

So with the confidence and arrogance I felt, I shouted, "Who is it?" I gave just as much authority as he did when he was banging at my door but more because this was my muthafuckin' house.

"It's Nick, can you open the door please?" He used his first name to convince me that he wouldn't be like the other cops I've known in my past. I knew it was bullshit because I just ran that same game on my son's girlfriend a little while ago.

I stood on my tippy toes, and saw it was a black dude, dressed in jeans and a clean white T-shirt with his badge dangling on his neck. I couldn't tell how tall he was until he backed away from the door and moved closer to the one across the hall. He was about six feet tall and looked more like a model than a detective, but I ain't give a fuck. I wasn't fuckin' him.

I opened the door with the chain still on it and said, "May I help you, Nick?"

"I'd like to come in, Ma'am. We *really* need to talk," he said with a meaningless smile.

"No."

"It's very important."

"I can hear you perfectly fine from here," I said as I mirrored his same smile with the same intensity. "So what do you want and please don't run game. I don't have time."

"Ma'am, I don't think you want your neighbors in *your* business. It would be in your best interest for you to allow me to come in so we can discuss this more privately."

"Why would it, *Nick?* You have probably knocked on every door in the building anyway. I'm sure my neighbors already know what you claim to be *my* business, although I don't know how true that is."

"That's not true." He lied.

"Nick, please," I said, growing bored with his games. "My son's girlfriend told me ya'll came around, so what you want with me now?"

He took a deep breath, clearly feeling defeated by my attitude and unwillingness to help him. *Good.* I had all intentions of wearing him down before he did me.

"I find that people who are uncooperative have something to hide."

"And I find that men who act like pussies are a *complete* waste of my time. I'm straight, so give it to me that way."

"You want it that way?" he asked as if he were threatening me.

"I want it that way!" I retorted as if I dared him to bring it on.

He took a deep breath and said, "OK, where's Delonte Knight, Mrs. uh … " He looked in his pocket and pulled out a folded piece of paper. "Mrs. Stayley. Where is Mr. Knight?"

"He ain't here. So what's your fuckin' point?"

"My point is, there's a lot of shit taking place in this unit. A boy was murdered and he appeared to have some type of affiliation with your son and *now* I've been trying to reach Mr.

Knight and have been unsuccessful. That's odd considering Mr. Knight has been very helpful to me. I mean, if your son knows as much as we think he does, your defensiveness would make sense."

"My defensiveness should make sense because you're getting on my nerves."

"And why is that?"

"Because you haven't said shit! Ya'll have been back and forth over here and haven't said anything worth hearing."

"Well I'm saying something now. Do you have anything to do with the disappearance of Mr. Knight?"

"Clean your ears because I'm only gonna say this once. I don't know shit, I ain't seen shit, and even if I did, I ain't telling *you* shit."

"Very ladylike, Mrs. Stayley. Very fuckin' ladylike."

"Good. I'm happy you think so."

"I do. I really do, but I hope you know that no matter what I find which may indicate otherwise, from here on out, my entire investigation will be against you and your son. You will take the fall for what I *know* you did to Charles and for what I *think* you did to Delonte. Trust me."

"Delonte, huh? So you two are on a first name basis?"

"What are you talking about?" he asked as he realized he should be calling him by his last and not his first.

"You know exactly what I'm talking about. I can't stand a dirty-ass cop."

"Have a nice day."

"Fuck you!"

When I closed the door, I leaned up against it and looked at my apartment. That muthafucka was on the take. I had a gut feeling that Delonte paid his ass to steer the investigation elsewhere, just as long as he remained safe. Now that I think about it, I remember him sayin' to someone on the phone, "As long as

I'm good, let things be good." Now I knew what that meant.

I couldn't believe the place I worked so hard to make a safe haven and call home for me and Kelsi wasn't safe anymore. I knew what Nick meant, too. He was going to frame us, whether we did it or not. The thing is, Kelsi did murder Charles and *we* did kill Delonte. But so fuckin' what! We committed both murders in self-defense, but I knew no one in their right minds would want to hear that, no one!

I knew if he dug around deep enough in my background, he'd see something emerge that would almost certainly convince him that I was capable of both acts, *alone*. He'd find out that I was a high-priced prostitute who was also the trophy piece to a big time drug lord, and a two-time felon wanted for murder.

When the phone rang again, I rushed to it and looked at the caller ID and smiled when I saw Lorenzo's name appear. Suddenly, I had one last murderous idea.

Kelsi
Chapter 18
September 29
Thursday, 8:05 am

With a fist full of money and a mean-ass dick stroke, I felt on top of the world. I ain't gonna lie, bangin' Kenosha's back out last night only fed my ego. 15 years old, and I had a 25-year-old bitch screamin' my name, *with* her Gramps in the next room. What was Kenosha's story though? Did she expect me to leave Keisha? If she did I wasn't down for that. Right now I wasn't sure what I wanted. Maybe I wanted to be by myself. All I knew for sure was last night I had some bomb-ass pussy. Since I hadn't felt the heat from the murders, right now, I considered myself to be one lucky-ass nigga.

Yeah, I was on top of the world but was broken down like G Money in *New Jack City* when I saw my girl cheesin' in Bricks' face. Don't get me wrong, I ain't no jealous-ass nigga, but what she was givin' in the hallway at school was a bit much. It didn't help that she was wearing a brand new outfit that I'm sure she bought with the money I gave her the other day. And the jeans! She knows I like to see that ass in skin-tight jeans, with them spiky boot joints and any top showing her titties. Look at that nigga, smiling like one of them retarded kids in room 2C. I should crush his skull.

Fuck that, I was 'bout to see what's up. When I walked over

to them, the moment she saw me, she broke down the hall.

"Keisha, Keisha! Come here girl!" I yelled.

She didn't come. Obviously, I wouldn't have played myself by yelling her name in the hallway if I knew she was gonna carry me, so I had to play it off, and hoped she was far enough down the hall so she couldn't hear me.

"Fuck you then, bitch!" I said as I waved her off.

I walked over to Bricks who was laughing his ass off against the lockers and said, "What's up with that?"

"I don't know man. I come in today and she comes up to me kickin' some bullshit."

"What bullshit?"

"Somethin' 'bout she was up all night watchin' *America's Next Top Model* and almost played hooky today from school."

"America's Next Top Model? What the fuck?" Bricks was talking but still laughing at how Keisha carried me, but truthfully, I ain't see shit funny.

"I wonder why she broke out on me like that."

"I don't know, man, but did you see how good your girl looked? Damn! Them jeans were made for her."

Like I said, ordinarily I ain't no jealous man, but even to a nigga who ain't give a fuck, that comment would've been too much to handle. I felt like knocking his fat ass up against the lockers, but I would have played myself, once again.

I said what I always did when we bullshitted, but this time I was serious. "Fuck you, nigga."

The expression on his face showed me he felt me, and I walked off to class.

Sitting in front of Keisha was hard because I felt the heat. She ain't say shit to me and I ain't say shit to her. I even walked over to this shawty who was feelin' me and whispered some bullshit in her ear. I was laying it on thick. Then I got a little carried away and started flirting with a few more and they were eating that shit up. Women are scandalous. They love to flirt with other bitches' men while they're watching. They were helping me play out my game real smooth. See, she forgot, I was still a wanted nigga even though I chose to fuck with her.

Keisha was shook, runnin' in and out of class asking to be excused and shit. She tried to play a game she couldn't handle. And now look at her, she got played. I was lovin' how fucked up she looked and then it dawned on me, she was mad because I ain't call her ass back last night. I was getting tired of her shit. If she wanted to act like a little girl everytime I ain't answer the phone, then she could suck my dick! I needed a woman. I wasn't about to start trippin' off a bitch. I was getting ready to be one of the richest niggas around, and if she missed out, oh well.

My Moms finally put it down to me about her reasons for wanting Delonte's weight, and I was feeling it. Makin' dollas, so we wouldn't have to be beggin' for shit, was something I ain't mind doin'. Besides, more money meant more broads, so as much as I was feeling Keisha, she could be replaced. Although I couldn't make Kenosha my girl, because she was empty-headed, I could still fuck her in the process.

Back At Home
4:15 pm
"I got it, Skully."

"You sure? I don't want to hear no bullshit, youngin'."

"I'm sure," I responded, tired of him doubting me. I never came up short with his money so I never understood what his problem was. "I ain't tryin to fuck wit you, or your money. I'll meet you about 9:15 by the corner store tonight. You got something else for me?"

"Yeah, and I'll give it to you later, but not tonight."

"Why later?"

"What I tell you 'bout askin' too many muthafuckin' questions?" He paused. "Don't!!!"

"Sorry, man."

"Don't be sorry, lil' nigga, just look out for your Moms. I'm out."

When I got off the phone I felt like I'd seen the devil. You see, Skully was never caught slipping until now. This nigga never expressed emotions. He was always the same heartless bastard I'd known since I met him. As far as I knew, he only gave a fuck about himself, so why the fuck he care about my mother?

When I heard her come home I was happy I wouldn't have to wonder too long. I decided to ask her straight up before she had a chance to get a story straight. I wondered what connection my mother had with Skully.

"So you know Skully, Ma?" I asked, not expecting it to come out like that.

The door closed, her eyes met mine and looked away.

The look on her face said it all. Whenever she was upset or nervous, she'd drop her keys on the counter, which she did, grab a drink, which she was doing and sit on the couch.

"What you talking about, K-man?"

"Ma, please stop calling me K-man. You always do that when you tryin' to remind me you my Moms. Trust me, I know you my Moms cuz it's the only thing I'm sure about, but I need you to be real wit me, like I've been real wit you. Do you know Skully, and if so, how?"

She took a deep breath and said, "Kelsi, come over here and sit down. We need to talk."

Oh shit. It's on. I knew now that whatever relationship she had with Skully was deeper than I thought. Prior to now I ain't even tell her I was pushin', but I was that sure she knew because of Skully's slip up. And if she knew Skully, she knew all about me. I sat in the recliner next to the couch so I could see her eyes.

"Remember our talk last week about there being a lot of things about me you don't know?"

"Yeah," I said, tryin' to guess how Skully connected with everything. "I thought you told me about your past."

"I told you almost everything."

"There's more?" I asked, already knowing the answer.

"There's a lot more baby."

"Like what?"

"Well," she said as she pulled in two deep breaths. "I was involved with a big time drug dealer in New York. I had everything, baby, and you were my son, so you had it all, too. Do you remember New York at all?"

"Not really, I remember hatin' the school and a bunch of flashy niggas runnin' in and out. Other than that it was too much goin' on so I'm runnin' a blank."

"Well, do you remember Jarvis? He was my boyfriend. He was out a lot but I thought you'd still remember."

"Not really, Ma. I had to be 9 years old back then, but you've mentioned his name like a hundred times when talking about Delonte. Sometimes you called Delonte 'Jarvis' by mistake, and I been meanin' to ask you about it."

"I didn't know I was doin' that. It's probably because they're both sneaky."

"Do they look alike?"

"No, but they have a lot of the same traits. I knew Jarvis had something else with him, just like Delonte, but I stayed in the relationship anyway. I do what most women do, let men use them up I guess." She looked away as she appeared to go somewhere else for a second.

There she went again draggin' the story out. Here it was, we committed a murder together, a crime so vicious we had no choice but to trust each other, and she was treating me like I was Cuba Gooding Jr. in the movie *Radio*.

"Ma, come on."

"I'm tryin' to, baby. This is hard for me."

"And so was killin' Delonte, but I did it."

"Eaaazzy Kelsi. Don't get fucked up," she said as she looked at me like she was gonna whoop my ass. At that time, having killed two people and everything, I was shook.

"Sorry, Ma."

"Like I was saying, I was keeping time with Jarvis. We were moving kilos of coke a week. I had so much money that I ran out of ways to spend it. I mean, a girl can buy but so many fur coats, purses and custom made jewelry pieces from Jacob the Jeweler. It was the life, Kelsi. After leaving your father who treated me like shit, I welcomed the lifestyle with open arms and a young heart. I was content but Jarvis was greedy. He told me he was able to get his hands on the same connect that Kyope, who was his best friend and supplier, used. He wanted to eliminate the middle man, which meant killing Kyope and making it look like a robbery. So wanting to please my man and prove myself like I did your father, I did what he asked me to."

I realized now why it was so hard for her to tell me. This sounded like some mafia shit, and I ain't imagine my Moms being involved in anything like this.

"He comes to me and asks me to frame Kyope by luring him into my bed. See, Kyope was always sweet on me but Jarvis ain't never want him to have me. Kyope didn't just want me, he cared for me. It's hard to say he loved me considering what he did to me later. But I can say this, his eyes told me everytime he looked at me, that at a different time and different place, if I chose Kyope instead of Jarvis, life would've been better for me and you both."

For real, I could do with out the sexual details she was giving, but I was listening anyway. My Moms was revealing a side of herself I didn't know about.

"So I did what he asked me to, I lured him to the hotel room. The plan was for Jarvis and a few of his boys to come into the hotel room to rob and kill Kyope once I had him there. But Jarvis told somebody and it got out, or it could have been that Jarvis told Kyope that I was setting him up and I was to be used as a sacrifice to prove Jarvis' loyalty to Kyope. To be honest, I don't know what happened. All I know is when I went to meet Kyope *alone* at the hotel as planned, Jarvis was there but he wasn't supposed to be. They were sitting outside together in Kyope's car in the parking lot waiting on me. I smelled deceit immediately!" The tears rolled down her face.

As I looked at my Moms tell the story, I knew she'd gone to that place and time. She was physically in the room with me but mentally she was where everything happened that night.

"So I doubled back to the house to get you from the babysitter but right before I was able to get out, they came after me. Jarvis acted like he didn't know anything about the plan. Even then, I wanted to protect him. I wasn't trying to tell Kyope anything. All I wanted to do was take you and leave," she continued as her tears and cries became mixed. "But he wouldn't let me leave. He wouldn't let me take my baby! He kept saying I had him fucked up for trying to set up his man. That I was wrong for trying to rob Kyope and had to pay with my life. I didn't really blame Kyope because he was right for wanting to kill me for trying to set him up but Jarvis knew he was in on it, and he didn't do anything to try and protect me!" she continued, wiping her tears. "They did a lot of shit to me including throwing me in the trunk of a car after shooting me several times in my shoulder."

I jumped up and looked at her. I always wondered where those wounds came from, but she was always sensitive when I asked her about them. Stuff was starting to come back to me. I remembered her sneaking into my room late one night and waking me up out of my sleep. Then I remembered her putting me into my closet and begging me to be quiet. *"Please Kelsi, be very quiet, baby."* Her face was wet with tears. *"Don't move and prove to Mommy you can be a soldier. Mommy needs you to promise."* And I did.

"You OK, baby?" she asked.

"Yes, go ahead, Ma." I sat down.

"Well, Jarvis and a friend had planned on killing me and dumping my body somewhere in a warehouse district but I got out, Kelsi. I got out and ran for my life. You were in the closet, back at the apartment and I prayed to God to keep you there. Safe. I ran all over but couldn't find my way out. I thought it was over, but then a man with a skull necklace found me, and saved my life."

I knew exactly who that was because he rocked that same joint now.

"Skully," I said as if it needed to be said.

"Yes." The tears falling down her face let me know that talking about it was too hard.

Now I wondered if the nightmares she had had anything to do with this shit. I wish I could find all of them and murder them muthafuckas one by one. I made a mental note in my head to never, *ever* forget the names Jarvis and Kyope for as long as I lived. I also developed a *new* respect for the man I worked for, but sometimes didn't like. After all, he saved my Moms.

I got up and handed her a tissue. Seeing her cry ripped my heart out. Shit! I was on some more murderous shit and I was trying to calm down. I felt like running outside and shooting anybody in my path. The only reason I didn't was because my mother needed me there. Going outside blazing wasn't doing shit but causing unnecessary attention and I needed to be focused.

"You don't have to tell me any more if you don't want to." I wasn't tryna hear no more shit but I was trying to be strong for her. I wondered how I was doing.

"I have to, baby. So after finding me and hiding me from Jarvis and that rapist –"

"They raped you?!"

"Yes."

Dead men. Somewhere on Earth were walking dead men.

"Go ahead, Ma."

"Skully took me back to our studio apartment in Manhattan, and you were still there." Her tears ran down her face and I knew they were mixed with the love she had for me. "Oh my God, Kelsi, you were there. Seeing your face was the best thing I'd ever seen. You didn't cry or make a move until you saw me, and then we ended up here. We could've been anywhere, but fate had it that we ended up here."

"Well now you're safe, Mama. I'll never let anybody harm you *ever* again! That's my word!"

"Well, baby, there's more. I did a lot of dirt when I was with Jarvis including killing two runners in the Cypress Hill projects in New York. So with this detective Nick coming by today, he's gonna cause a lot of problems."

"Nick Fearson?" I asked.

"I don't know. I didn't get his full name."

"Well when I told you about the blackmail, I didn't tell you Delonte wanted me to push coke for him, cuz at the time I ain't want you to know I was pushin'. But he was blackmailing me by threatening to tell him everything and he said he had the shirts covered in blood."

"Shit! We forgot to burn them!" she yelled.

For one minute we realized we made a crucial mistake that could cost us majorly.

"Well I was right about the blackmail being drug related. I was right about Nick being on the take. This is not good. He came by and threatened to dig in my past and if he does, he'll uncover all that shit I told you and more. Now Kelsi, jail time I can handle, but that won't happen. The moment he starts sneakin' around, he'll find out my alias is Helena Hope, and Jarvis and Kyope may come lookin' for me to finish me off. We got to get out of here."

"Well let's do it! What we waitin' for?" I said, ready to dump all that bullshit and be out.

"We don't have enough money to hide deep enough. I got 15 grand saved up and I know you got some too, but unless you hiding a hundred thou, we won't get very far."

"OK, so what's your plan?" I asked, sensing that she had one. She wasn't all hysterical and shit like I was, so that made me feel better. A *little*.

"It involves one last murder."

What was she sayin'? We already had two murders under our belt, which were far from being blown over, along with the heat from her past. Killing somebody else made no sense to me. It was like running down the street with gasoline drawers on.

"Ma, what are you sayin?"

"I'm sayin' this last murder will give us enough money to live comfortably. With enough to build an empire on the lifestyle that stole our freedom. What I'm sayin' is, Kelsi, we should kill your father so you can cash in on his life insurance policy."

I can't breathe. I'm trying to but I can't. I had asthma when I was little but it hadn't bothered me in years. As a matter of fact, I remember the last time it happened was in the closet when I heard them beating her and she was screamin' for her life. I probably blocked it out of my mind. I don't want to think about that shit now. The only thing that saved me was remembering her telling me to *Breathe Kelsi, breathe. Take your time and breathe, Kelsi.* And I did. In the closet, alone, and in the dark, I breathed until I saved my own life. It's amazing what comes back at the strangest times.

A lot of shit my mother said always carried me through. Like the night I was fighting for my life with Charles. If it hadn't been for me remembering something she said to me, that nigga would've taken me out. Now as I thought about her words, I realized I could breathe. The thing is, what am I breathing for?

Janet
Chapter 19
September 29
Thursday, 10:15 pm

"Shelly, I can't tell you why, I just need you to promise."

"You know I'll take care of Kelsi if something ever happened to you, but if you trust me enough to do that, the least you could do is tell me why," Shelly quizzed on the other end of the phone.

"For once, can you be a friend to me and not Lorenzo? I should be able to count on you and still maintain some level of privacy."

"Whatever, Janet. Once again everything is about you. Well don't worry, Kelsi will be taken care of in the event anything ever *happened* to you."

I knew I couldn't trust Shelly as far as I could throw her, but I felt good she'd do right by Kelsi. With everything going on, anything could happen, and if it did, I wanted to have a back-up plan. I had even written a letter confessing to both the murders and would write another one which would include Lorenzo if need be. I was willing and ready to take the fall for everything including the murder of Charles. I felt confident that if I were killed within a year, Kelsi would be more than able to take care of himself, but if they took me out now, I wasn't sure. Where my only son was concerned, I needed to be *sure*.

177

"Shelly, if everything was about me, why would I ask you to look after my son?"

"Are you in trouble?" she asked, ignoring my question. "Or are you about to do something you ain't got no business doin'?"

"If I was, would you really want to know?" I said, trying to scare her. I knew she didn't have a clue of the life I really led because if she did, she'd be scared to death and she certainly wouldn't be asking me any questions.

"And what is that supposed to mean?"

"Nothing, Shelly. I'm sorry," I said, realizing it was stupid to irritate the woman I was entrusting to look after Kelsi if I died.

"It's cool, but Janet, how come you didn't ask Lorenzo? I mean he is Kelsi's father."

You see how I was trying to spare her feelings, right? I was convinced that the day I invited her into our bed, I introduced Lorenzo to someone more loyal to him than his own mother. I wanted to say something to shake her up, since she was always concerned about him. "How you know he'll *always* be around?"

"Real cute, Janet. Did Kelsi like the stuff I brought over for him?" she asked, doing a terrible job of trying to change the subject. Her voice was shaky and everything. Life without Lorenzo was totally unimaginable for her.

"Answer the question."

"Janet, please. Lorenzo will always be around."

"Are you certain? Is he invincible or something?" I asked, picking at her wounds. Lorenzo was the right and left crutch for her and without him she would fall apart.

"Janet! What in the fuck is wrong with you! Stop it! Please!" she said as if she were about to start crying.

"OK, OK," I said, reducing my voice.

"Did Kelsi like the things?" she asked, repeating the original question before I got maniacal on her.

"I guess so," I said, trying to save her from further embarrassment. "He pulled the tags off and wore most of it out of here. Hey, I gotta go. Kelsi just walked through the door."

"OK, Janet. Tell him I said hello."

"I will."

When I got off the phone I wanted to talk to Kelsi about my plan for Lorenzo, but I'd given him so much already. I felt it would be best to put things off until later. But on the other hand, time was something we didn't have a lot of. I ran into the kitchen and scooped his plate up and placed it on the counter. Afterwards, we met in the living room.

"Hey, Ma," he said as he walked in, gave me a kiss on my cheek, and sat on the couch. "I just came back from meeting Skully, and I thought of something else I wanted to ask you."

"OK, shoot," I said, sensing uneasy urgency in his voice.

"How come you let me sell dope?"

"Kelsi, is that what you think?" Sitting on the recliner in front of him, I prepared to answer his question. After all, everything that had happened recently appeared to be condoning violence and crime.

"Well, you knew I was pushin' and you allowed it. You knew I murdered dude and you helped me cover it, and then we go out and kill Delonte. So I'm wonderin' was makin' me a killer your plan all along?"

Whoa ... pump the brakes. That hurt. Kelsi's comment tore through me and hurt me to the core. I had to gain my composure because my first instinct was to reach out and smack the shit out of him.

"Kelsi, first off you're wrong. Dead wrong. No mother wants to see her child hurt or hurt anyone. I tried my damndest to protect you from the streets and the pressure out there. Why you think I took that second job? To give you things so you wouldn't have to resort to this lifestyle, but I had to prepare myself if you chose that path. Am I wrong for having a plan just in case you chose this life anyway?"

Silence.

"You were a victim of circumstance, so how could this have *always* been my plan? I ain't hold the weapon in your hands when you took out Charles, that was all you. I wasn't on the corner with you pushin' dope. That was all your doing. Delonte had to be killed because he was an accessory to the fact, so what we stood to earn a little profit! People earn profit all the time by the death of others, it's called life insurance!"

"So why you let me run for Skully?"

"I *let* you run for him cuz you were gonna do it anyway. You're a product of your environment, Kelsi. You didn't think I saw the fire in your eyes and your desire to want more? You got in honest! I was the same way, too, and I'm *just* realizing that I'm still like that today. If I told you to stop you would've done it anyway. Why not put you in contact with someone who'd look after you? When you're a hustler it's in your soul and there's nothing nobody could do to change that. So Skully promised me that he'd always look after for you, and to never give you more than you could handle. I took Skully's word on that. Another reason I took the part-time job was just so I could save a stash just in case I saw something in your eyes which told me you needed me if you came up short or somethin'. Everything was planned out to the 'T'. Skully looked out for you and Delonte knew it, so when I told him he was blackmailing you, and that I believed it had something to do with his product, he cut his ass off. End of story."

"But you said Skully caught you runnin' from the people you set up. It ain't ever cross his mind that you weren't trust-worthy?"

"I'm gonna say no," I answered, building myself up to explain something that most people couldn't and wouldn't understand. "I think he knows I'm loyal. I was loyal to Jarvis but he wasn't loyal to Kyope or me. He tried to play both sides. He'd tell me how much he hated Kyope and wanted to do business on his own, but then he'd tell Kyope that I was greedy and stayed in his pockets. That's just like me being best friends with two people who can't stand each other. It just ain't possible. Although I helped set up Kyope, it wasn't because I was disloyal, it was because I was very loyal to Jarvis."

"But do you believe in your heart that Skully trusts you?"

"Yes I do."

Kelsi got up and walked over to the fridge. He grabbed a soda and poured it down his throat. I knew he wanted some liquor, but I wasn't ready for all that, even with the murders he committed.

"So Skully knows about the murders and everything, huh?"

"No. He knows about the one with Delonte, and he thinks you had something to do with Charles but that's only because he knew about the fight."

"You said trust no one."

"I know, and don't," I said, meaning every word. "But how could I not have some level of trust for the man who saved my life? He could've taken me out a long time ago, but he didn't."

"I guess you right," he said with a slight smile.

"I think I am."

"I'm sorry Ma, I never doubted you. I got a lot of stuff on my mind. I think Keisha is slidin' around on me. I just needed to hear a few things. It seems like when things fall apart in some places, they start fallin' apart everywhere.

"I know baby, and that's why I wanted to be honest with you."

"Thanks, Ma."

"But Kelsi, I wanted to talk to you about her, too. I saw her talking to Bricks at the IHOP off of Bladensburg Road today."

It was true. Today she called me upset at how Kelsi was carrying on at school, so I suggested she meet with Bricks and talk about her problems with him. I even suggested the place and everything; so although it was all my idea, I really did see them together. He walked over to me and sat down.

"Ma, please don't say that. Please tell me you just didn't say that," he pleaded as he kept punching the inside of one of his hands with his fist. Kelsi did that whenever he tried to prevent himself from crying or showing any emotions. "Please tell me that's not true."

He was hitting his right hand so hard, I thought he would break it. At my own risk, I placed my hand in his, knowing he wouldn't strike it, so he couldn't hurt himself anymore.

"I can't tell you that, baby. I can't tell you that because it *is* true. I started not to say anything, but when you mentioned her name to me, I took it as a sign."

He took his hands, dropping mine and started rubbing the sides of his head as if it were a crystal ball. I knew he was trying to understand everything that was goin' on. I wanted to hug my baby and tell him I loved him because I did, but the bottom line was, this was the life we were dealt, and there was no getting out of this game. Being in love and feeling hurt would be the least of our problems. I felt bad for him, but I rather he be hurt right here with me, than out there in front of her.

"Ma, I ain't want to tell you 'cause I cared about Keisha, but that nigga came after me because of her. So in a sense, all this is her fault, and now I'm finding out she slidin' with my boy! I'm sorry for putting you in danger because of this. I'm sorry for everything."

My hate for her just increased. But before I could get fully pissed, he said, "Ma, I gotta go! I gotta do something real quick."

"Kelsi!" I shouted as I jumped up and blocked the door.

"What are you getting ready to do?"

"I'm getting ready to kill that dude, Ma. He played me! He smiled in my face like he was my boy, and he's doin' my girl! She got me murderin' muthafuckas because of her. This is all her fault!" he yelled as he punched his hand over and over again. "I even seen them this mornin' smiling in each otha's face. They did that shit in front of me! I was thinkin' at first that she was tryin' to make me jealous, and at first I wasn't trippin', but now … now I feel like both of them played me in front of everybody. They probably laughin' at me right now."

I could tell he was fightin' back tears and I think it made him madder that he was about to cry. I needed to do something to calm him down and keep him in the house. If he left, he would be a one-man army and destroy whatever crossed him. In an even-toned voice, I said, "Baby, what I tell you about outside influences? We have too many things to worry about now. We have a plan to stick to, so let's stick to it. Use that hate! Use it!!"

He looked up at me with rage in his eyes. I knew he was thinkin' about his best friend holdin' or having sex with his girl and had changed those feelings to hate to fuel his fire.

"I'm ready, Ma."

"Ready for what?"

"Ready to hear your plan."

Kelsi
Chapter 20
September 30
Friday, 8:15 am

The first thing I saw when I walked in class was that bitch wearing a royal blue dress, spiky boot joints, with her legs wide open. I guess she had gotten over her little mood, and expected things to be cool, but I *still* hated that bitch. She was fucking my boy and I was hittin' that raw. Dead man was right about that slut. She probably sucked his dick, too. I realized she did the same thing to me that she did to him, except we weren't friends.

She hopped from nigga to nigga each year. Last year it was Charles, this year it was me and next year it'll be Bricks. But she ain't about to make me look stupid. I was cuttin' that bitch the fuck off.

"Hey baby, I called your cell last night. Did you get my message?"

Silence.

"How long you gonna be mad at me?"

Silence.

"Come on, Kelsi. I miss you!"

Silence.

"Why you actin' like this? Why you still mad at me?"

Silence.

I hoarded that bitch through the entire first period.

A Hustler's Son

When one of Keisha's archrivals came over and whispered in my ear that she was having a party, Keisha damn near lost it. Carmen's titties almost fell out of her shirt and everything. It was the perfect ending to my day. I heard her sniffling in the back of my head and I didn't give a FUCK.

I was happy when the bell rang, too. It was just a matter of time before her fake-ass tears got on my shirt and I wasn't tryin' to get dirty. The moment the bell rang she ran up to me.

"So you fuckin' with Carmen?" she asked as she ran up behind me. "Kelsi! Are you fuckin' with Carmen now?!"

Maybe something on the back of my gray hoodie gave her the impression that I gave a fuck because she kept talkin' to it.

"Kelsi, I'm serious. I don't think I can take this. I can't live without you," she pleaded as she walked in front of me.

"Bitch, I'm done wit you. It's over! Get the fuck out my face!"

I was straight givin' it to her, and every time she begged, it made me madder and madder because that's how she used to get me. I bought her anything when she cried but now I'm finding out that she seduced my boy just cuz she was mad at me. That nigga Bricks would have never had a chance with a girl like her. Don't get me wrong; I ain't fuck with him either. He was wrong as hell, too, but niggas will be niggas, and I don't know if I'd be able to turn down a girl of Keisha's caliber if the shoe was on the other foot, but at least I'd try. I mean, we had just broken up and already he was laying pipe to my bitch.

"Kelsi! I'm not leaving you alone!" She yelled loud enough to make a scene in the hallway, trying to make me look cruddy for carrying her. I didn't care because she was makin' herself look worse, and since she wanted to act stupid, I decided to give it to her.

Niggas started to gather around to see what was happening. Bricks walked over through the crowd fakin' like he ain't know

185

what was goin' on. I used to know shit was all good when I saw his face but now he was my enemy, too.

"Bitch, didn't I tell you it was over? So why you still in my face? I'm done wit you!"

I looked into the group of niggas who were still watchin', ready to scrap if I hit her. I noticed a lot of faces were those of niggas that were sweating Keisha since we first started kickin' it. I also saw faces of niggas who I fought because of something she said or did. That fueled my anger even more.

"Who's next with this bitch? I'm done with her!!" I yelled as I pushed her hard into the group of nosey-ass niggas and I walked off.

In the halls after school

Bricks had already come up to me tryin' to feel me out. He thought I was trippin' off of him sayin' something about Keisha's jeans, but he didn't know I knew everything. That stingy muthafucka ain't take nobody nowhere so the whole IHOP thing was blowin' me. *"I know you ain't getting mad cuz I said something about how Keisha looked in her jeans man. We play all the time,"* he reminded me. Fuck that nigga! I left that fat bastard in the hall because I was tired of him blocking my view.

I was almost out of the building when Lakeisha walked over to me. She was out of breath and already crying.

"Listen Kelsi, before you say anything, just listen to me. I love you."

"Oh my goodness! Why are you stalking me? First your ex-boyfriend, now you!"

"Kelsi, I'll do anything you want. Please don't do this to me. Don't do this to us. We been together forever. I don't want nobody but you!"

I had the baddest girl in school begging me. Damn! It seems

like when you treat a bitch right they carry you, but when you treat 'em like shit, they stay on your dick. So if she wanted to beg, I decided to do one last thing before cutting her ass off … for good.

"Tell me the truth. You sucked Charles off in the lot at the Plaza, didn't you?"

"If I tell you the truth you gonna be mad." She was cryin' and I already knew what the answer was. For real I ain't want to hear it. I just wanted confirmation that the bitch does lie and that most of all she was a whore. Damn, she was a fucking whore!"You want me?" I quizzed, thinking about what I knew she did.

"Yes baby," she said, smiling like I asked her to marry me.

"Come here," I said as I walked toward the boys' bathroom holding her hand.

"Where we goin', Kelsi?"

"You askin' questions?" I said, giving her the impression that she'd be cut off with the quickness if she said yes.

"No."

"Well get the fuck in here," I said, pulling her into the boys' bathroom.

I walked into one of the stalls, and opened the door. Without asking any questions, she came right in behind me. Once we were in the stall, I unzipped my pants, made her get on her knees on the nasty-ass floor, and told her to suck my dick.

"You know what time it is."

"You gonna be with me after this?"

"Yep," I said, lying my ass off.

"You promise?"

"What I tell you about askin' a million questions? Don't!"

"OK Kelsi, OK."

Let me tell you something, she sucked my dick so good, that for a second, just one second, I was considering taking her ass back. I mean balls and all were in her mouth. But it's funny what you remember when you love somebody and they do you wrong. I asked this bitch the night I murdered that muthafucka what happened. What really happened. And in my bed, next to me, she lied to me. It's all good though. Because right now, she was sucking my dick like her life depended on it. In the boys' bathroom, on her knees, she was giving me the best head of her life. She should be commended for that shit. Right when I was about to bust, I pulled my dick out and bust all over her face. I ain't even want her swallowing my babies.

When I was done, I acted like she wasn't even there. She ran to the sink to wipe off her face and I walked right out the door. It didn't take her long to come after me.

"Kelsi! Kelsi! Can I come with you?"

"No, bitch. I told you, I'm done with you."

"You dirty fuckin' dog!! You would make me suck your dick and carry me."

"I ain't make you suck shit. You got on your knees your muthafuckin' self. I ain't gonna lie, I lost respect for you after that shit. Do you realize that only five percent of the piss gets in the toilet and the rest hits the floor?" I laughed. "You a nastier bitch than I thought."

"Kelsi!" She was crying so hard she was really starting to make me wonder why I ever liked her to began with. I mean for real, she ain't have no heart. I thought she was a ride or die chick. I would have given her some props if she said, "FUCK YOU, KELSI!" or something. A bitch this weak could get me killed.

She ran up to me and got in front of me. "I can't live without you, Kelsi," she cried as she grabbed me.

"Well die bitch! Do something, anything, but please get the fuck out my face."

For some reason I felt like I ain't never have any feelings for her anymore. Whenever I felt sorry for her, I thought about her doing the same things we did with Bricks. If she was that quick to suck my dick on the bathroom floor, who knows what else she might do with him or any of these other niggas in this muthafucka.

Just then my phone rang, "Yeah. I'm coming out now."

When Keisha saw Kenosha's Benz pull up, she fell down, grabbed my leg and started crying. I kicked her off and started walking away. I was almost to the car when she said, "It was your mother! It was her fault!"

Hold up! What was this bitch gonna say about my mother? Was I gonna have to kill her ass? I walked up to her and grabbed her hair. Kenosha got out the car like she was getting ready to do something.

"Do I look like I need your help?!" I yelled at Kenosha. She shook her head no. "So get back in the fuckin' car."

When she did, I directed my attention back to the slut who, in one second, was getting ready to have a broken neck if she said the wrong thing.

"What did you say about my mother, bitch?"

"Your mother, Kelsi!" Her speech was fucked up because she was crying and trying to catch her breath.

"What the fuck did you just say about my mother!"

I didn't care. That slut ain't deserve to breathe my mother's name let alone say it. I started to think about all the things my mother did for me and how this slut, after one argument betrayed me, and I slapped the shit out of her. She fell to the ground tryin' to get away from me. I caught up with her ass and slapped her again.

"Please Kelsi! Please, I'm sorry," she said as she tried to run back into the building on her knees.

I caught up with her, and with visions in my head of her fucking Bricks and thinking about her disrespecting my mother, I beat her ass in the front of Bladensburg High school. When I was tired I lifted her head by the hair, her face was drenched in blood and I said, "Were you sayin' somethin about my mother, bitch?"

"No Kelsi, no, please no more," she cried as she laid her face in the grass. "I thought you said you'd never hurt me, Kelsi!" she repeated over and over. "I thought you said you would never hurt me."

"I *said* I'd never hurt my girl, but I could care less about a slut," I said as I let her go and left her right there in front of the school as I rolled out with Kenosha.

A Hustler's Son

Where the fuck was Moms at? Something ain't right. I ain't feelin' this shit and I knew in my heart something's wrong. We went over the plan a million times last night. She would get in contact with Lorenzo, tell him she was thinking 'bout letting me slide at his place from now on, and then we would *all* meet me out here so we could handle our biz. So where was she at now?

When I looked down at my phone I noticed Bricks had called me six times. All that did was irritate me. There's nothing like waiting for somebody else to call, having your phone ring, and it be somebody else. Anyway, I didn't know what I planned to do with him yet. It was still to be determined, but if he called during the same time my Moms did, and she wasn't able to reach me, that would be another reason for me to hate his ass. He called six times and ain't leave a message until the last time. I wasn't tryin' to hear shit he had to say, but I needed to listen to somethin' because thoughts in my head about what was goin' on with her started to drive me crazy.

I called my voicemail and I heard him say, "Man, this Bricks. You need to get up with me for real. Keisha tellin' me your Moms got me mixed up in some shit I ain't have nothin' to do with. I need to clear my name with you, and I want to do that

191

shit in person. I ain't the one to do you cruddy man and I ain't about to start now. I know this a misunderstanding so get at me."

What the fuck was he talking about? He was probably tryna cop a plea, and what was Keisha talkin 'bout? Damn, that bitch was crazier than I thought. She tryin' to put my Moms in the mix on whatever shit she got goin' on with Bricks, but I ain't havin it. I shoulda did everybody a favor and let Charles keep that bitch.

When I looked down at my watch, and saw she ain't called me yet, I was getting more and more noid. A half an hour had passed since she said she would be here with Lorenzo and nothin'. Maybe he found out we were trying to set him up! Shit! But how could he know that? It doesn't make any sense!

But how come she wasn't at Haines Point where she was supposed to be? My legs were shakin' and my head was beatin' like a drum. I looked like I was on that shit. I shoulda walked up to his ass, blasted his head off, and left my Moms out of it. The plan was supposed to be simple, murder his ass, throw him in the ocean and cash in on his million-dollar life insurance policy. If he fucked with my Moms I'm telling you, I would do him worse than Charles and Delonte combined.

"God, I haven't prayed to you in a while and for real, I felt I wasn't worthy. But you can't take her from me now, I know you know that. I read the Bible and I know that some of the greatest battles ended in bloodshed, and for a good purpose. Please let me handle this and I promise that I'll never murder again, at least I'll try not to."

I was sittin' in another rental when I noticed a familiar pair of headlights, and one was cracked. It looked like the same car I'd seen at school sometimes coming to pick up Keisha, but what the fuck was it doin' here? When I saw Sparkle's car pull up beside me, I ducked down in my seat. I ain't have no time to be kickin' it with her cackling ass. What I saw in Sparkle's car made me reach for my piece because it wasn't her. Instead it was one of the maddest bitches I seen in a long time, and she was lookin' dead at me.

She parked the car on the right of mine, so I couldn't drive away. There was a car in front of me, in the back, and now hers on the right. The railing was on the left so there was no place to drive. I was blocked. If my Moms called me right now sayin' she needed me, I couldn't move, and that made me want to slap her ass all over again.

"So you wanna carry me and shit? That's how you wanna carry shit, Kelsi?"

"What the fuck you talking about, bitch? And what in the fuck are you doin' here?"

"I'm talkin' about your smack party you had on my face and how you rolled out with that bitch."

"I told you it was over, bitch, so why are you here?" I got out the car and approached her.

"I followed your ass and was waiting for your little princess to show up. I got tired of waitin' and decided to pull up on you cuz I know what goes on at the Point. My Moms used to play this spot all the time. Don't nothin' go on here but a bunch of fuckin', so where she at, Kelsi? She realized you weak as all get out and left you stranded?" She laughed.

"Keisha, get the fuck out of here! Now is not the time, I'm tellin' you!"

"Kelsi, why don't you love me no more?!"

"I can't believe this shit! Are you serious! You pick now to come up here and talk to me about some bullshit?!" I said with both of my hands on my head. I couldn't believe Keisha was going out like this.

"Why in the fuck are you doing me like this, Kelsi! Tell me that?!"

"It's over! I'm feelin' somebody else!"

"Who Ke-no-show? Where she at, Kelsi?! I was waiting for her too so I could fuck her up! If she think she gonna get my man she got another thing coming."

"Get the fuck outta here with that bamma-ass shit! I'm done with you, slut!"

"And I'm done with you. Your dick some garbage anyway!"

I looked around and was glad there wasn't anybody around us. That's why we chose the Point to begin with. My Moms said it used to be jumpin' all the time and at one time, you couldn't even ride through let alone park a car, but now it was isolated and quiet. That was, until this bitch showed up and started wilin' out.

"Yeah right, bitch! My dick some garbage huh? That's why you following me around and shit? Yo Keisha, for real you betta get the fuck outta here before I –"

"Before you what, Kelsi? Before you fuck me up? I don't give a fuck no more! I did what your Moms told me to do and I lost my man. As far as I'm concerned it's that bitch's fault not mine."

Bang Bang Bang! She was already down but I shot her again. *Bang!* Killin' her was the easiest. All this shit was that bitch's fault! Charles was after me because of her, we had to kill Delonte because he knew about it, and now my Moms was missin'. *Bang!* If I never met her I wouldn't have to do any of this shit.

Damn! I had to get rid of her body. I picked her up and pulled her toward the water but she was still movin'. I got up on her head. *Bang.* She wasn't movin' no more. I ain't see nobody near me and so far, it looked like only the ocean was a witness, so I gave her to it. Swish.

When I ran back to the car I realized I was still blocked in. Just because I killed her didn't mean I got rid of the problem. And her keys, where in the fuck were her keys? I looked in the car and they weren't there. I looked on the ground and they weren't there. Then I remembered that bitch put 'em in her pocket, and now the keys were at the bottom of the ocean. *Oh snap!* Now the rental car was gonna stay blocked with Sparkle's shit. I ain't know what the fuck I was gonna do now.

I called my Moms over twenty times and she ain't answer her phone and I knew I couldn't stay around there any longer. Shit was too hot for me there. Although I ain't think nobody saw me shoot her, there was always a nigga in the corner watchin'. *Remember, the streets are always watchin, Kelsi.* Damn! Where was my Moms? I decided to start walkin' and hit up Kenosha for a ride. I had to help my Moms before things got out of hand. I was positive that something was wrong. But I wasn't saying it out loud. If I said it out loud, I would have to admit it and I didn't know what that meant.

The phone rang a few times before she finally answered it. "Hello, Kelsi." Her voice sounded different than it had in the past. "Where are you?"

"Ummm, I need a ride. I'm at the Point. Can you slide through and pick me up? I'm by the statue of the man coming out the ground." I was amped, nervous and worried. Now I realized that the triangle of emotions I was feeling was a deadly combination.

"I'll be there the moment I get through with matters here." *Click.*

There was somethin' in Kenosha's voice that sounded cold as shit. For one thing, she wasn't soundin' all ghetto and draggin' out sentences and she wasn't excited to hear from me like she was earlier. Everything about tonight was different and I was startin' to get noid. As long as my Moms was safe, I could still do what needed to be done, but if she wasn't, I ain't know what I was capable of.

"Mama if you can hear me, I love you. I need you to know

I love you," I said as I dropped to my knees and realized my worst nightmares were coming true.

"Mama if you can hear me, I love you. I need you to know I love you." I thought I was dreaming when I heard Kelsi's voice. That was until I woke up. I wonder if this is what Delonte meant when he said there's something I have to tell you. Maybe dead men don't tell lies. My eyes were swollen shut. I could barely see through one of them, and I only tried to open the other when I heard him talking to me. It hurt too much otherwise. I was sitting on a cold floor with nothing on but my bra and panties. My back was up against a pole and my hands were tied behind my back.

Once again I'd been taken away from my home, and I still wasn't sure how he got in. It was as smooth as if he lived there. The last thing I remembered was preparing to meet Lorenzo, so Kelsi and I could handle business. The next thing I knew, I was being forced into a scenario I hadn't planned for. *A scenario I hadn't planned for.* That sounds so weird because I plan for everything. I try to teach Kelsi to plan for every possible scenario too, but never in my wildest dreams did I see this one coming.

Kelsi, I'm so sorry baby. I'm so sorry for this life I've gotten you into. Please forgive me. I wish you could hear me. I feel

your love. Can you feel mine?

"Helena Hope, you ready to die?" He interrupted me from my thoughts.

"Yes," I said trying to form full sentences even though my lips were split and twice their size due to constant punches. "Please don't hurt my son. He ain't have shit to do with this."

"I know he didn't. This all you, Helena. You should've stayed out the game. I tried to warn you, but you didn't listen."

"But he was blackmailing my son! I had to fuckin' kill him!"

"Blackmailing him for what? You lied to me, Helena! You told me he was blackmailing him to fuck with my product. You knew how I felt about that shit! But it wasn't true, was it? He was blackmailing him because he knew he killed that dude."

"He didn't kill him. I did." I was spittin' up blood and my stomach hurt because he used it as a punching bag. Getting punched in the stomach and hit in the eyes were pains I could do without, and he did both of them over and over again.

"You're lying but it's cool. I'm not the fuckin' cops but you should know that all of this is your fault."

"I know, oh God I know," I said, crying so hard every muscle in my body ached. "And I'm ready to accept my fate. All I ask is that you spare Kelsi's life."

"But Helena, it's been about Kelsi all along."

He was calling me by my alias trying to remind me of my past but lately I thought about it every day.

"I don't get it. What do you mean it's all about Kelsi?"

"I mean, the night I saved you, I knew exactly who you were but you didn't remember me. Maybe if you weren't so scared you would have. I don't know, and to be honest, I don't give a fuck," he said as he circled around the pole I was tied against. His voice sounded like surround sound speakers that ripped through me.

"There was a party one night that you and your man gave. You were supposed to make *all* of his associates feel comfortable. You were so high that night that honestly, I didn't know it was possible. Poppin' those E pills had you fucked up. Anyway, you all high and shit, took one look at me and said, "I ain't fucking that black muthafucka. I can't even see him." You thought you were hilarious. My friends laughin', and Jarvis' friends laughin'. I was the butt end of your muthafuckin' joke!"

I was tryin to remember that night but I couldn't. Maybe he had me confused with someone else and this was all a mistake. Please God, let it be a mistake.

"Maybe it wasn't me because I *honestly* can't remember."

"Shut the fuck up and listen! That's your problem, you wanna be a man so much you *love* disrespectin' one. Well I'm not Jarvis, bitch."

I was so scared that I couldn't move. The warmth that came down my leg felt comforting at first, and then it started to run cold. Here I was, on the floor, sitting in my own piss, realizing I was about to die. To top it off, I had to worry about Kelsi being unsafe. I wished it was a way to tell him how much I loved him. I wished it was a way to tell him how proud he made me. But in my heart, I felt he'd never know. I kept *many* journals when I stayed with Jarvis and one at the apartment in Maryland. I wanted him to have them because I talked so much about him. But I'm sure Skully would never give him anything from the apartment.

"Like I said, you said to me, 'I ain't fuckin with that nigga!'" See, I wasn't worried 'bout it for real. You had already fucked five dudes that night and I wasn't feelin' like standin' in line to be number six. Still, I ain't appreciate how you played me in front of my boys and I ain't appreciate how Jarvis ain't put you in your place, but I didn't expect him to because I never liked that nigga. Anyway, I was going to the bathroom and went to Kelsi's room by mistake."

"Lil' shawty looked right at me and said, 'What up nigga!' I kicked it in his room for a minute just shootin' the shit. He had a personality. I thought about the kind of person you were and how you had him around all that shit, so I made a pact with him. I told him just as long as I'm alive, he'd be safe. You know what he told me? 'Just as long as I'm alive you'll be safe, too.' You think he'll keep his promise now?"

Silence.

"Anyway, he said it with passion in his voice and everything! So when I saw you all fucked up that night, similar to what you look like now, I saw an opportunity to make good on my promise. I mean, its not his fault his mother's a whore. I figured he was somewhere by himself that night, and I needed you to go get him. I just didn't know where he was. Trust me, I would have killed your sneaky ass myself that night."

I was weak. I couldn't believe Skully had plotted against me this entire time. He was never down for me. Once again, somebody I trusted turned on me, but I still wasn't understanding the *reason* for wanting Kelsi! Was he tryna make him his son or what? It didn't make any fuckin' sense. What hurt the most was the last thing I said to my son regarding Skully was that I trusted him. He asked me if I trusted him. He probably sensed something was up and I said yes, I trust him. Damn!

"You left us, I mean you left Kelsi without nothing for the first few months we moved into the apartment in Maryland. If you were so down for him, why you do us like that."

"Janet, who in the fuck you think sent Delonte? I did. That's why he was so persistent, I kept sendin' his ass back. I knew he wasn't no good but I needed somebody to look after Kelsi and I needed somebody to keep an eye on you. He did everything I told him to besides fuck you with my dick."

Damn. That would explain why I always felt he never

belonged to me. Like he was a robot or something.

"But what do you want with Kelsi? I *still* don't understand." I was crying but the tears couldn't fall from my swollen eyes, and the ones that did burned my face.

"I want his passion!! Do you realize you have created a fuckin' killin' machine? I can have him do anything for me in *your* name. See, the last thing you said to him was that I saved your life, so when you're gone, who do you think he'll trust?"

"Skully, be real wit me! What in the fuck do you want with Kelsi?" I screamed, not caring about the pain in my body. The pain in my heart took over that in my body. He wasn't telling me shit. All I gathered was that he met Kelsi and wanted to look after him, but why?

"OK, since tonight is your last night alive, the least I can do is tell you the *entire* story." He laughed. "I'm tired of Jarvis' shit! Do you realize I found out that this muthafucka was skimmin' off the top of product I bought from Kyope? I found out that muthafucka had been doin' that shit for years! I go over Jarvis' head to Kyope, tell this muthafucka what was happenin', and he tells me he'll talk to Jarvis, like we fuckin' brothers and shit! This MUTHAFUCKA STOLE MY SHIT!!! Now the nigga stopped hitting my pockets, but what about all the money I could've made? A pound of coke every time a drop is made adds up to thousands. Now normally I'd murder his ass myself, but he's Kyope's right hand man, and I ain't tryin' to fuck up my connect, but if Kelsi does it, nobody will suspect him."

"But why would Kelsi go after him? That shit happened years ago!"

"Because I'll tell him it was Jarvis who pulled the trigger tonight."

"Skully, you could pay somebody to take out Jarvis and then you wouldn't have to get Kelsi involved."

"But it won't be any fun. Do you realize how much money

I'd pay to see Kelsi kill that nigga?"

"Fuck you, you bastard!!!! I can't believe this is happening. Please wake me up. This is not really happening! If you gonna kill me go ahead cuz I can't take this any more!"

"Not yet. I have one last treat for you. I want you to meet the person who'll look after Kelsi while you're gone."

When I heard female shoes clicking, I tried to open my eyes. I couldn't see shit. I needed to see the woman who would be in my son's life forever. Maybe if she could see me, she'd take pity on me and be easy on Kelsi.

"Hey Jannneeett! Ooooo I'm gonna take such good care of Kelseeee!" she said sarcastically.

"No!!!!!!! Not Kenosha!!!!! Nooooo!!!!"

"And just so you know, I'm very educated, bitch. I play dumb for those who like it that way."

This is not happenin'. This is just like all those other bad dreams I've had in the past. I'm reliving a nightmare I didn't even know existed. Please wake me up.

"Janet!"

"What do you want, Kenosha? If ya'll gonna kill me, get it over with! I was dead the moment I found out Skully turned on me. And you, you got rid of that shit at Delonte's house didn't you? His mother didn't do it."

"Yes, sweetheart. Who else do you think did it?" She started laughing hysterically. "I can't have you gathering all of the product and reselling it to Skully, can I? It was his anyway!"

"You's a no good-ass slut!! Both of you are grimey!"

"And you should know what one looks like," she said as she slapped my face.

It didn't hurt. I was too angry to feel any pain.

"So what, you gonna try to put the moves on my son now, bitch? He won't ever want you!! I taught him how to find a snake. He smelled you the moment you introduced yourself."

"No baby, I don't want your precious baby boy. I'll just have a little fun with him. I'm Skully's leading lady."

"That's right, Janet," he said with a confident tone.

"How you gonna be anybody's anything?"

"I'm just like you were, only better." She laughed. "You played the game but played it wrong. But it was nice knowing you," she said as she cocked the gun. "And don't worry about us getting back in your place, I got the keys."

"Kelsi, I love you!!"

"Good night, bitch!"

Click ... Bang! Bang! Bang!

Pulling for breath ... pulling for breath. Isn't it amazing how life turns out? The same man who saved my life. *Pulling for breath.* Just ended it. *Breathless.*

Kenosha
Chapter 23
October 1
Saturday, 11:35 pm

Janet was a funny bitch. She tried to call me out on the same game she played, only I played it better. She fucked to get what she wanted just like I did. Delonte used to tell me how stupid she thought I was. Everybody's not ignorant just because they act dumb. I am to people what they want me to be, and what they *need* me to be. Delonte needed me to *want* him, cousin or not, and I gave it to him. The only blood I care about is running through my veins. If you can do something for me then I can do something for you. If not, keep steppin'.

People love to say Kenosha ghetto, *so I bees real ghetto and shit and if they really likes it, I may even start actin' like a baby so I can really get what I want,* but I'm highly educated, with a degree and everything. Fuck a degree! The moment I got it I wiped my ass with it. I like a thug nigga, with a thug mentality and fast dollas to go with it. In turn, I'll talk when they say talk, move when they say move, just as long as the money flows in like a fountain from a well. Bottomless baby. That's the only way I like it.

So Janet didn't know shit, but I'd keep an eye on Kelsi, it was just a matter of time before he'd be eatin' out my hands, too. Mark my words, and for collateral, I'd hold on to these blood-soiled shirts and Janet's journal. I guess I'm not too dumb, cuz not even Skully knows about these.

Skully
Chapter 24
October 4
Saturday, 11:50 pm

I do what I do because I do it! End of story. I don't owe nobody shit and I don't expect nothin' but for my money not to be fucked wit! But that nigga Jarvis got me fucked up along time ago. I hate a crook-ass nigga. He too sneaky to be in the mutha-fuckin' game, so when I see his bitch beggin' at my feet, why not take the opportunity to get revenge? It won't get the money back in my pockets, but it will wet them with his blood. I ain't lie about makin' the lil' nigga a promise. I did, and I'll look after him until my work is done, and then, he's dead too. He knows too much. When he kills Jarvis, I'll blast him.

There was no need to tell Janet all that. She was a hustler. I'll give her props on that, but in my opinion she should've stayed out of the game. She had no business fucking around in this lifestyle again. I hate to give it to her baby boy, but I have to. It'll be my way of looking out for Kyope by takin' out the nigga who killed his right hand man.

In the end, I'ma be the last muthafucka standin'. Believe dat!

Kelsi
Final Chapter
December 26
Monday, 1:45 pm

A Greyhound bus pass and a backpack is all I'm takin' with me. It's all I need. I packed three bottles of water, four Snickers bars, a pack of condoms, six wife beaters, eight boxers, twenty grand in cash, the two framed pictures of my Moms and a pistol. Destination? New York City. I don't look at it like I'm runnin' away from home because home died when my Moms was killed.

I can't say I know *exactly* where I'm goin' but I know what I'm gonna do. I have enough information to find who I'm lookin' for, or to get 'em pissed enough to come lookin' for me. I don't give a fuck how it goes down just as long as we get it over with. The way I look at it, I ain't got shit to lose. If I die I'll be with my mom, but if I live, they'll have to kill me because I won't rest until I hunt down his ass along with anybody he fuckin' cares about.

For two months I've been dealin' with my mother's death only to realize I ain't dealin'. Getting up in the morning, still expectin' her to come out and say, "Good Morning, K-man," even though I asked her not to call me that. What I wouldn't give to hear her call me K-man now. What I wouldn't give to hear some advice.

You ain't felt alone until you walked this Earth without your mother. See, at any time your pops could get mad, walk out, and you'd never see his ass again. See, muthafuckas expect them to roll out because that's what they do. People base *their* love on whether or not support checks come on time or not. I guess if that be the case, I can say mines ain't fuck with me at all, but your Moms ain't got no option to roll or to not support your ass, she gotta do it. At least mine didn't. It was me and her against the world. I could do anything with her by my side.

Some people may think I'm fucked up but I don't give a damn. Murder is a way of life, and I rest easy knowin' that one day, I'm gonna die, too. Good! Take my life! I want to see my Moms. It's the cycle of things. How you gonna live on this Earth if muthafuckas don't move over and die? It's gotta happen, but before I die, I'm gonna take out every muthafucka who ever made my mother cry, pops included.

And that night, that night was like a fuckin' nightmare. When Kenosha slid by to pick me up from the Point, I ain't have no idea of what was in store for me. That nigga completely demolished our apartment. Ripped shit up. Broke shit. Took shit. It was fucked up, and worst of all, my mother wasn't there, not even her body or no signs of it.

I called the one person my mother trusted, Skully. He told me that Jarvis probably had something to do with it because of that Nick dude drummin' up shit. He figured word probably got back to them New York niggas that Moms had moved to Maryland and they sent their hounds. I believed him. I believed it was all Jarvis' fault, because even if he ain't kill my mother with his bare hands, he was still responsible for all the shit he put her through. He set my Moms up, left her hanging and shot her twice, but she still ain't die! Somebody should've told that nigga that a true soldier lives forever!

Hell, she even took the fall for my murders. She wrote a

note and had someone mail it if she ever came up missing. In it she confessed to the murder of Charles, Delonte and even what she referred to as the "Murder at Haines Point." It worked out perfectly because a few days later, Lakeisha's lifeless body washed up at the Point and the rental car I used was still parked in the same spot. I always wondered how she knew not to include Lorenzo's name on the confession. I knew the murder at Haines Point was supposed to be for Lorenzo but instead it ended up being for Lakeisha.

Maybe it was the same instinct that told her to tell Shelly to look out for me so that bum ass Lorenzo couldn't do it. Or maybe it was because she didn't see it done and wanted to be sure first. I don't know what her reasons were, but she looked out for me, and her confessions allowed me the freedom to avenge her death! I know I sound like a super hero, but I don't give a fuck. She kept me free so I can free her, and because of it, they don't know the time or the hour I'm comin', but I *will* be there.

Since I ain't never see her body, I held onto the hope that maybe she wasn't dead, but on Christmas Day, I was delivered a package I'd never forget. I was sitting in the living room with Lorenzo, Shelly and Lorenzo Jr. They were opening gifts but I wasn't in the mood. The doorbell rang and it was a FedEx delivery person with a package for me. When I sat and opened it, it rocked me. My mom's heart was in a box with a note sayin' "*Nobody has heart when they're dead.*"

I couldn't cry. I had shit to do and tears would blur my vision. It was obvious they wanted beef by disgracing my mother's name so I decided to bring it. I was stayin' with Shelly so rollin' out was too easy. I told her I had some things to take care of and when I'm done, I'd be back and if I'm not, *don't* come lookin' for me.

The next thing I did was call Skully. He told me he understood what I had to do and why I had to do it. He even told me a few places to look for Jarvis and Kyope. Real helpful, right? I know. A little too helpful for me. When I thought about all the things he did for us I remembered what she used to tell me, *"Nothin' is as what it seems."* The more I thought about it, the more I had a feelin' she was right. I'm not sure if Skully is down for me, but, but I do know that only time will tell.

The next thing I heard was like music to my ears. "Ladies and Gentlemen, Welcome to New York City."

ORDER FORM

Triple Crown Publications
4449 Easton Way, 2nd Floor
Columbus, Ohio 43219

Name: _____

Address: _____

City/State: _____

Zip: _____

	TITLES	PRICES
	Dime Piece	$15.00
	Gangsta	$15.00
	Let That Be The Reason	$15.00
	A Hustler's Wife	$15.00
	The Game	$15.00
	Black	$15.00
	Dollar Bill	$15.00
	A Project Chick	$15.00
	Road Dawgz	$15.00
	Blinded	$15.00
	Diva	$15.00
	Sheisty	$15.00
	Grimey	$15.00
	Me & My Boyfriend	$15.00
	Larceny	$15.00
	Rage Times Fury	$15.00
	A Hood Legend	$15.00
	Flipside of The Game	$15.00
	Menage's Way	$15.00

SHIPPING/HANDLING (Via U.S. Media Mail)   **$3.95**

TOTAL $_____

FORMS OF ACCEPTED PAYMENTS:

Postage Stamps, Institutional Checks & Money Orders, all mail in orders take 5-7
Business days to be delivered.

ORDER FORM

Triple Crown Publications
4449 Easton Way, 2nd Floor
Columbus, Ohio 43219

Name: _____

Address: _____

City/State: _____

Zip: _____

	TITLES	PRICES
	Still Sheisty	$15.00
	Chyna Black	$15.00
	Game Over	$15.00
	Cash Money	$15.00
	Crack Head	$15.00
	For The Strength of You	$15.00
	Down Chick	$15.00
	Dirty South	$15.00
	Cream	$15.00
	Hoodwinked	$15.00
	Bitch	$15.00
	Stacy	$15.00
	Life	$15.00
	Keisha	$15.00
	Mina's Joint	$15.00
	How To Succeed in The Publishing Game	$20.00
	Love & Loyalty	$15.00
	Whore	$15.00
	A Hustler's Son	$15.00

SHIPPING/HANDLING (Via U.S. Media Mail)   **$3.95**

TOTAL $_____

FORMS OF ACCEPTED PAYMENTS:
Postage Stamps, Institutional Checks & Money Orders, all mail in orders take 5-7
Business days to be delivered.

ORDER FORM

Triple Crown Publications
4449 Easton Way, 2nd Floor
Columbus, Ohio 43219

Name: _____

Address: _____

City/State: _____

Zip: _____

	TITLES	PRICES
	Chances	$15.00
	Contagious	$15.00
	Circumstances	$15.00
	Black and Ugly	$15.00

SHIPPING/HANDLING (Via U.S. Media Mail)   **$3.95**

TOTAL $_____

FORMS OF ACCEPTED PAYMENTS:

Postage Stamps, Institutional Checks & Money Orders, all mail in orders take 5-7 Business days to be delivered.